Replicated Murder

A Medium with a Heart

Book 2

Erica J Whelton

Publisher: Sunseri Design Publishing
ISBN: 978-1-956069-03-7
Second Edition

Printed in the United States of America

To my wonderful husband who has put up with a lot as I focus on this story. Thank you for all the support.

3

And a special thank you to Dominic for giving me the serial killer's nickname. It fits perfectly!

Books in this series:

Premedicated Murder (book 1)
Replicated Murder (book 2)
Organized Murder (book 3)
Inherited Murder (book 4)
Crafted Murder (book 5)
Destined Murder (book 6)

Other books by this Author:

Mandy's Story: A Glenn Lake Novel (book 1)
Becca's Story: A Glenn Lake Novel (book 2)
Caroline's Story: A Glenn Lake Novel (book 3)

The Haunting of Anna-Rose (Paranormal Suspense)
Decoding Us (Women's Fiction/Friendship)

Chapter One

~ Stalker ~

My heart hammered as I walked past her house again. Three times now, and still no sign of her. If I didn't catch a glimpse soon, I'd have to leave before some nosy neighbor called the cops.

Damn Karens.

The cops were the last people I wanted to see. A few questions, a little digging, and I'd be in serious trouble. I had too much to hide and everything to lose.

I sighed and turned toward home. A few blocks back to my car, then a ten-minute drive.

One last look. Just one glimpse. But instead of her, a car pulled into the driveway.

Crap.

Detectives Walden and Hartley climbed out. They wouldn't know me, but I knew them. Time to go.

I continued toward my car, keeping my pace casual. No need to draw attention.

I'd come back another day. Until then, I'd have to find someone else to satisfy my craving.

~ Joanna ~

I cradled Oakley in my arms as she cooed happily. We'd bonded quickly over the past two and a half months since I adopted her.

Her backstory was complicated. Her mother, Cate, had kidnapped me while I investigated a pharmaceutical executive's murder. Turned out Cate was the murderer. She went into labor during my captivity and switched from killer to terrified single mother. She asked me to be her labor coach and, afterward, to adopt her daughter. She knew she'd be going to prison for life.

Strange how labor, birth, and adoption could make us friends. My life was so weird.

"You have a sad backstory, little one, but together we'll have a bright future."

Oakley rewarded me with her sweet, toothless grin. Her newest skill, and it melted my heart every time.

"I never thought I'd have this," I whispered.

When my husband Ted died, I'd thought all hopes of motherhood died with him. Nobody had told me about the smiles, though.

I checked the clock. Close to naptime, and the detectives would be here soon.

In my office, I peered out the front window. No car yet, but a guy walked by, pausing in front of my house. Looking for something, maybe? I hadn't seen him before. New to the neighborhood?

Oakley squirmed in my arms, getting tired.

"Okay, sweet girl, let's get you in a fresh diaper and down for your nap."

Movement outside caught my eye. The detectives pulled into my driveway.

"Sorry, you'll have to wait." I rubbed her back as I headed for the door.

"Good afternoon, detectives."

"Afternoon." Clint nodded.

"Hi, Joanna and sweet Ms. Oakley." Terry wagged his finger at her.

She stared back with wide blue eyes before flashing one of her baby grins.

"Please, come in. I need to get her changed and down for a nap, but y'all can have a seat in the living room. Feel free to help yourselves to drinks."

They followed me in. I turned right toward Oakley's room while they went left to the kitchen. I could hear them whispering as I changed the baby.

"Sleep sweet, baby girl." I laid her down, checked that her monitor was on, and quietly left.

In the living room, Clint scratched at the wrapping on his water bottle while Terry perched at the edge of my dark blue armchair, whispering something. Clint's bouncing leg and Terry's drawn face made me anxious. Whatever brought them here was causing them stress.

"Thank you for meeting with us. Sorry about the timing." Clint nodded toward Oakley's room and cleared his throat. He looked at Terry before continuing. "We were hoping with your success solving the Landon Labs case, you could help us with another one."

"I'm not sure how. That was mostly luck. Plus, I don't want to change my whole business. I'm a medium, not a detective."

"I know, but that's exactly who we need right now," Clint said.

"Have you been contacted by any spirits who mentioned being killed by a serial killer?" Terry asked.

"No, not yet anyway."

They shared a disappointed look.

"Okay, thanks," Clint said.

"I'm willing to try, though. I don't want to put myself back in danger like with Jeremy."

Clint shifted in his chair. "We don't want to involve you too deeply or put you in danger, but we keep hitting a brick wall. Before this guy kills again, we want to try any source we can. We don't know who else to ask."

"Agreed. We definitely don't want to put you in danger again, especially now with Oakley in the picture, but if we can use you as a consultant, we think it would be helpful." Terry added.

I looked around the room at the many spirits present. During the daytime, my house was always full of them. Some hoped I could contact their loved ones. Others waited for their scheduled appointments.

Thankfully, they cleared out at the end of my workday. Privacy was rule number one with me.

None stepped forward, so I looked back at the detectives.

"Without contact with at least one victim, I'm not sure I can help, but I'll try." I thought for a moment. "Can you give me any information? It might help me get started."

"We can tell you some things that have been shared in the news. We can't give you confidential details." Terry said.

I nodded.

They shared what they could—names, some family members, and how they died. Much of it I could probably find online, but I took notes anyway.

They didn't want to share much about the deaths, but I pushed for details. Drugged, tied up, and tortured until they died.

"Yikes, that's awful. So cruel, but it helps me understand what I'm getting into." I jotted more notes. "I'll see if I can get one of them to meet with me, somehow."

How to call them? It wasn't like the dead had cell phones. I'd tried meditating and focusing on specific spirits before. Sometimes they appeared, but my success rate was maybe eighty-twenty. More coincidence than actual summoning.

I scanned the room as the dead people started chatting among themselves, trying to figure out if any knew the victims. Too many voices talking at once. Maybe that would be the key—getting this ghost network on my side.

"We really appreciate your time." Terry stood while Clint remained seated, staring at me. Terry tapped his shoulder and nodded toward the door. "We'll get out of your way."

"Yes, thank you for your time," Clint said, standing.

I walked them out. Clint hesitated at the door as if he wanted to say something else, but instead nodded and followed Terry.

I locked up behind them and checked the time. About an hour until the baby woke. Time to research the victims.

Firing up my computer, I started with the first victim, finding numerous news articles. She'd been reported missing and found a week later. Killed in the most gruesome way. I shuddered reading the details.

I searched for the next victim and the next. They all looked roughly the same. Dark hair, dark eyes. Between 5'2" and 5'4" tall, a few extra pounds, all in their mid-twenties to early thirties.

The hair on the back of my neck stood up. All the victims looked a lot like me. At least in basic features—not enough to be mistaken for twins, but enough to set my nerves on edge.

When Clint and Terry gave the description, it hadn't clicked. I vaguely remembered them mentioning it months ago when these murders started, but seeing the faces triggered my anxiety.

Likely a coincidence, but I couldn't shake the paranoia, especially given Grams's warning about someone still wanting to harm me. Had this been who she meant?

I flipped through their pictures again, staring at each face.

"Wow, this is eerie."

The silence broke with my daughter's faint cries—almost like kitten meows—as she started waking. She'd be ready for a change and a bottle.

I pushed her door open. "Hey, baby, did you have a nice nap?"

I changed and fed her, then carried her to my office to continue researching. Easy at this age to hold her while I worked.

Next, I looked for connections between the victims beyond physical appearance.

Ashley worked at a small law office. Lindsey was a vet tech. Laura and Emma worked at retail shops, but not the same one. Brittney was a waitress, and Jalynn worked at a daycare. The last victim, Bethany, was a teacher.

None seemed connected by friends, family, or jobs. I had to dig deep to find any mutual friends.

I didn't know much about psychology, but from what I did know, serial killings weren't usually random. Typically there was some connection. What it was with these women, I had to figure out.

After an hour or so, I couldn't look at the computer any longer. Time to make dinner.

"I can't figure this out." Oakley squirmed in my lap. "Yeah, I know. I didn't expect to figure it out in one night, but I hoped to find some clue."

She smiled in reply.

"A girl of few words. I like that."

As I stood from the computer, a new face stepped into the room. With so many spirits coming and going—though they normally quit around this time—I was rarely surprised anymore.

"Excuse me. You're Joanna, yes?" the ghost said.

"I am, and you are?" I recognized her from my research. "Oh, you're Lindsey, right?"

"That's right. I heard from some of the others you were asking about me."

"Yes, I was. The officers investigating your death—I'm sorry, by the way." She shrugged. I smiled before continuing. "They asked if I had contact with you. I said no, but that I'd try."

"I wish I could help. I honestly don't remember much. He grabbed me from behind. I never saw him. He injected something into me. The world started spinning, and that's all I remember until I woke sometime later. No idea how long, but when I came to, I was tied and blindfolded. What I do remember is him ranting a lot while he tortured me."

"Ranting?"

"Yeah, he kept saying things like 'She never notices me' and 'Why doesn't she care?' Weird stuff like that. I didn't understand what he was talking about. Thankfully I was heavily drugged, so I don't remember much else." She spoke calmly with no hint of anger or fear. I'd think either response would be more appropriate, but she seemed at peace. "Once he started cutting me, I passed out, and that was it."

"You seem almost at peace with this."

"I was upset at first, but it's strange how being dead shines a new light on things. I can't do anything about dying, so why stay upset? Plus, it was months ago. I've had time to adjust." She smiled. "But if I can help find the killer, I'm happy and willing to do that."

I nodded. I didn't know how I'd react if I was dead. When Cate had a gun to my head, I didn't like that. Had she succeeded, I can't imagine I'd be accepting of it.

"Do you happen to know any of this guy's other victims?" I asked.

"I'm not sure since I don't know who killed me. Only what I heard from the cops when they found my body. My spirit was still in the room. They said they thought we were killed by the same person—the 'Playhouse Killer,' as the media's calling him—but even they weren't sure at the time."

"That's true." I thought for a moment. If she couldn't give me information we didn't already know, she wasn't going to be much help. "Well, thanks for coming. If you remember anything else or meet any of the others, please let me know."

She smiled before turning to leave. Oddest conversation I'd had in a while. It didn't give me much additional information, but at least I knew she hadn't suffered. I wondered if the other victims had been so lucky.

Chapter Two

~ Joanna ~

That night a huge storm blew through. Thankfully, Oakley slept through it. Unfortunately, a tree fell on my patio, taking out the pergola and half the deck. Wind blew debris across my backyard and took down part of my fence.

"What a mess," I mumbled, surveying the damage.

I walked to the front yard. My oak tree had only lost a few small branches, and some trash had blown in from somewhere. Not as bad as the backyard, at least.

Up and down the street, neighbors inspected their homes. Some had minimal damage in the front, but the neighbors three houses down had a tree through the roof.

The entire street was littered with storm debris. It looked like a war zone. Everyone seemed as stunned as I felt.

While I stood there trying to decide my next move, a handyman's van pulled up at the curb. I'd seen him stop a few houses down to talk to neighbors. Painted on the side was Donovan's Handyman and Yard Services.

"Hello, ma'am. I'm driving around to see if anyone needs help with storm damage." His eyes scanned my front yard. "Did you have much more?"

"Yes. A tree fell in the backyard, damaging my patio and fence. Then these branches in the front." I nodded toward the name on the van. "Are you Donovan?"

"Yes, that's me." He smiled proudly and climbed out to shake my hand. "Do you already have someone working on it, or do you need an estimate?"

I hesitated. This seemed too easy, but it would save me time finding someone on my own. I didn't even know where to start looking for someone to do this work. What was the harm in having him check it out?

I looked him over as he stood there waiting. Thinning auburn hair with touches of gray. Stocky and short. Maybe five-nine. Muscles showed under his short-sleeved shirt, suggesting he was strong and worked his arms, even if the rest of him looked out of shape. His face was worn with age but not too old. Perhaps early to mid-fifties. His smile was warm and friendly.

"Yes, I'd love for you to take a look Jand give me a quote."

"Great." He grabbed a tool bag from the front seat and followed me to the backyard. "Wow, you sure did get some damage. Okay, let's see." He examined the structure, then started measuring and writing in a small notebook. I stood back, feeling helpless. My beautiful yard was trashed. I'd worked hard to keep it maintained. I'd imagined that as Oakley got older, I'd set up a play set under this tree for the perfect amount of shade. We'd have tea parties or dance parties on the deck.

Now those visions had changed. The deck could be replaced. A new tree would take years to be big enough to fill my dream.

"Okay, so you're looking at about two thousand for the whole job. Not including labor, which will add another three hundred. But that does include taking out the tree, repairing the pergola, deck, and fencing."

Not as bad as I'd thought. "Oh, wow. When can you start?"

"I could start immediately." He put his tape measure away. "I have one other house, but they asked me to start later today, so I have time now to at least start the cleanup."

"Really? That would be great." This was easy.

"I'll start hauling this out, then grab lumber and begin the repairs, probably tomorrow." He looked around the yard. "Or the next day."

"Do you need a deposit or anything?"

"No, ma'am. I'll collect full payment at the end of the job."

Perfect. I nodded. "Thanks. I'll let you get to it."

I went back inside to check on the baby, even though I was holding the baby monitor. I was still in the checking-that-she-was-breathing stage of motherhood, which made me look a little obsessed at times.

I had clients scheduled today. My nanny, Janie, would be coming in, plus my assistants Tessa and Micah.

With the storm last night, I'd checked on all three to ensure they were safe. Janie and Tessa were both okay, no problems, but Micah had a tree down in the street blocking him from getting out. He and his partner, Josh, were working on getting it cleared with the help of another neighbor. He said he'd be in once the road was clear enough.

I went to the kitchen to rinse the baby's last bottle and grab another cup of coffee. I peeked through the curtain to see how the work was coming along. He'd already gotten a large portion of the tree cut.

Wow, that was fast. I took a sip of coffee as I watched him work.

He paused a moment and looked at the house. Something in his expression sent a chill down my spine, though it seemed like an absurd reaction. I was thankful he couldn't see me from where I was standing. He only looked for a brief moment before going back to work.

I shook off the feeling as silly paranoia.

Stepping away from the window, I made my way to my office. I wanted to get in a little research on Lindsey before work.

Even though I'd already done that and talked to her, I wanted to dig into more personal information versus the news stories. If I could get more of a feel for who she was, maybe I could find clues to the killer.

I found her old social media accounts. My lucky day. They were open to the public.

She was a pretty girl with what appeared to be a loving family, had been engaged, and looked to be a social butterfly. Tons of pictures of her traveling or at clubs and parties. Vastly different from my own life.

I rarely went out, choosing work and staying home, particularly now. Though I did spend time with my family and a few close friends like Micah and Tessa.

Message after message of love and I miss yous for Lindsey. Some brought tears to my eyes. I couldn't imagine if I lost someone close to me, like my sister or one of my assistants. I'd worked with them for years. They were like family to me.

"Knock, knock," Janie said, announcing her arrival.

Perfect timing. I was starting to hear Oakley stir, and I'd have my first client shortly.

"Good morning. It sounds like she's starting to wake. I was about to go get her, but now you're here." I smiled.

Chapter Three

~ Joanna ~

The next day was more clients. My life was fairly predictable that way. I worked a lot, but I enjoyed my job, so it wasn't a chore. I got to help people, both dead and alive, find peace, giving them last messages of love and support. It was rewarding, though at times being so close to death could be depressing.

A good team around me helped. Adding Janie for Oakley was a blessing. I always thought I had fairly good instincts about people. Unfortunately, like anyone else, I got it wrong sometimes, but overall, not bad.

When Janie arrived that morning, Oakley was awake and in a playful mood.

"Hey, Janie. Here she is." I handed my daughter to her nanny.

"Oh, how's my favorite girl today?" She cooed to Oakley. "Are you ready for a fun day?"

Oakley giggled and cooed in reply.

"She has a new diaper and had a bottle about thirty minutes ago."

"Okay, great. We'll head back to her room for story time." She waved the baby's hand at me. "We'll see you later, mommy."

I turned into my office. I had to review a few checks and invoices Tessa left for me to approve and sign. Micah had also left his proposal for our next merchandise order, and I wanted to review it before he arrived so he could place the order today.

I was head down working when there was a sound by the door. I jumped.

"Oh, I'm sorry. I didn't mean to startle you." The spirit said.

"No, I'm sorry. I was so into what I was doing." I recognized her from my research. "Emma, right?"

"That's me. I heard through the ghostvine, get it?" She laughed at her joke. I smiled. "Anyway, I heard you wanted to talk to me."

"Yes, I was hoping you could tell me more about who might have killed you. Maybe who it is? If you knew him?"

"Yeah, I had a feeling it might be about that. I didn't get a great look at him. He grabbed me from behind and drugged me with something."

"So, not even a glimpse?"

"Not really. A reflection in a window, so maybe I could describe him a little."

"Oh, great." I picked up a pen, ready to take notes. "So, is he tall or short?"

"Tall, definitely." She scrunched up her face. "No, he was short but taller than me. Maybe five-nine or five-ten? Do you think that's short or tall?"

"I don't know. Medium?" I said. "Um, okay. What about his build? Fat, fit, muscles, or thin?"

"Thin with muscles." She screwed up her face again.

"Are you sure?" I asked.

"No, you're right. He was fat."

"Okay, so a fat man a little taller than you."

"Yes, and he was almost definitely bald and had a mustache."

I started to write it down. This was frustrating.

"No, wait!" She exclaimed. "Darkish hair and thick but thinning in the back."

She was exhausting. I wasn't getting anywhere with her.

"What about the mustache? Yes or no?"

"No, clean-shaven. I'm sure of it."

"Okay." I wrote what she said, even where she changed her mind. Any description was better than none. Well, almost. I looked down at my notes. This could be anyone. I tapped the pen a few times and then looked at her.

"Maybe I don't remember it as well as I thought, but it's weird when you die. Details of your death are blurry. I remember my childhood, my family, and my friends. I remember my job, but I don't remember much about the man who took me or even where he took me."

"I guess I've heard that from some others."

"Yeah, despite the violent way I died, it was oddly peaceful."

"Really?"

"Yeah, I simply floated away." She smiled and stared straight ahead, then shook her head. "Also, he'd drugged me heavily. It messed with my mind."

"The other victim I spoke to said something like that too. She said she was at peace." I put my pen down. "I'm so sorry."

"No, no reason to be sorry, and I've been dead for a while now. I mean, I'm bummed in some ways, obviously, but I am at peace." She shrugged. "My life was crap before. Working retail? Being screamed at by customers. My boyfriend had ended things with me because he was sleeping with my sister. Men are pigs. Both parents were dead already, so I didn't have much. I'd hoped things would have gotten better, but now I am free, and it doesn't matter anymore!"

She threw her arms out and turned her face upward. "I'm happy. I stick around to see what my ex and my sister are up to. I haunt their house. It's so much fun." She giggled.

"Well, okay. I appreciate you sharing. If you can think of anything else, or hear of anything, would you let me know?"

"Of course. By the way, I think it's really cool what you do. I have talked to a lot of ghosties. They're happy with the peace you've given them. I don't have anyone still alive I care about, but ya know, still think it's cool." She waved, leaving as quietly as she arrived.

I sat there staring at the place where she once stood. I couldn't believe what she said. Having met a lot of dead people, while most were at peace in many ways, she was the only one so far that was happy to not have closure from anyone left behind, except for her haunting some of them. It made me sad for her life.

I heard a car pull up and saw it was Donovan. I went out to greet him.

"Good morning, Donovan." I waved as he got out of his van.

"Mornin', Ms. Joanna."

"I didn't get to see you before you left yesterday, but I wanted to tell you I was impressed with all you got done. I'm so glad to have found you."

"Thank you. I was happy for the work."

"I'll let you get to it. I have clients shortly anyway." I went back to the house and got back to work, reviewing paperwork and meditating before my first clients arrived.

Before I knew it, my busy workday ended. Between the work going on in the backyard, wonderful clients, and all the paperwork I had to go through with my assistants, the day flew by. I loved these days because it got me to the fun stuff.

At nearly three months old, Oakley was close to rolling over, so I spread a blanket out in the living room to let her stretch out and help her work on it.

"Here ya go, baby girl." I held a toy in front of her.

She reached for it but couldn't quite control her arms.

"Almost, Oaky. You can do it."

She tried again and again missed it. She made a few frustrated sounds but tried again. On that try, she rolled to her stomach, looking up at me with surprise.

"You did it!" I clapped. She smiled up at me, but she started crying. "Oh, no, don't cry. It's okay."

I scooped her up, rubbing her back, speaking to her softly. Once she was calm, I put her on the ground again. We continued playtime until there was a knock at the door, interrupting us.

"Now who could that be?" I looked down at Oakley. She should be okay for a second while I go to the door, so I left her playing. I peeked through my office window. It was Clint. "That's odd."

"Hey, Detective," I said as I opened the door. "Everything okay?"

"Hey, Jo. Yeah, yeah. Sorry to drop in. I just..." He looked down at his feet and back to my face. "Um, can I come in?"

"Oh sure, come on in. Can I get you a drink?"

"Oh, no thanks. I'm good."

We walked back to the living room, where the baby was happily playing. She had moved from her original spot in the middle of the blanket and was now on the edge of it. How did that happen? I guess things were going to get really real soon. Sooner than I thought.

"Oh, hey, Ms. Oakley." He squatted down to be closer to her face. She rewarded him with a huge baby grin. "Awe, she's cute."

He stood and looked at me. I gestured for him to sit.

"So, what's up? New stuff with the serial killer case?" I asked.

"No, but have you had any luck by chance?"

"Actually, yes, sort of. Two of the victims have contacted me now, Lindsey and Emma. I didn't call you about it because they didn't have any usable information on the case. Nothing you didn't already know. Emma tried to give me a description, but honestly, what she gave me could be any middle-aged man in Creekview."

"Darn. Oh, well, maybe one of the others will come forward."

Chapter Four

~ Clint ~

I was reviewing the missing person report on Victoria Sellers. The kindergarten teacher had been reported missing a few days ago by her parents when she didn't come home after a night out with friends.

We had no clues, and a review of security cameras in the areas showed she left the club they had all been at. Two of her party went in one direction, she went the opposite way, entering a space that couldn't be seen by the camera, and that was it. Gone.

I looked at my whiteboard where I'd written out several names, victims of the Playhouse Killer, as the media was calling him. I could only guess that this was going to turn out to be another one.

"I hate this guy," I said to the whiteboard.

"Talking to yourself again, Hartley?" My partner, Terry, strolled in and took a seat in my extra chair.

"Just reviewing this missing person file."

"Ah, yeah. Think she might be a victim of the Playhouse Killer?"

"I hate to even think it, but yes." I fidgeted with the edge of the file. "This guy is slick. How could he not be visible on the cameras? They are everywhere."

"It appears he understands how and where the cameras are pointing," Terry said.

"Hartley. Walden." Our supervisor stuck his head in my door. "Tip on the missing teacher, possibly out by the airport. A white van was seen in the area with a man and woman in the front seat. Woman fits the basic description."

"Okay, great. Was there a specific area? There are easily fifty buildings in and around the airport." Terry pointed out.

"West side. Was all they said." He handed Terry the tipster's name and contact information. We would connect with him once we got to the airport.

"It's better than nothing." I grabbed my keys and stood.

Terry and I headed out to the airport. First, we went to the mechanic shop to talk to a guy named Jude.

I parked, and we got out. I glanced around. This was one of a dozen buildings on this street. Most were abandoned and falling apart. If he didn't have concrete information, we were going to end up on a wild goose chase, but some information was better than none.

Before we made it inside, a mechanic came outside to greet us.

"Hey, there. Can I help y'all?"

"Yes, we are here to meet with Jude," I said.

"Oh, yeah, he's in here." The man said, "Hey, Jude."

"Yeah?" came a voice from inside.

"Guys here to see you."

A lanky mechanic in dark coveralls came out. He was wiping his hands on a rag, then adjusted his ball cap. "Um, can I help y'all?"

"We're here about the tip you called in. I'm Detective Hartley. This is my partner, Detective Walden."

"Ah, yeah. Okay. Yeah, so I saw that teacher chick that is missing. She was with a big guy. Young with a neck tattoo. They drove past me, and the guy asked for directions. They went towards the terminals." Jude said.

I pulled out a picture of Victoria. "Is this who you saw?"

"Um, oh, no. This chick was blonde or like a light color, could've been gray. But not like silver-gray, but like blonde-gray. I thought the victim was blonde, and the lady I saw was older. Like sixty or maybe seventy, even."

"So, you're saying you didn't see this person." Terry pointed to the picture.

"No, I guess I didn't see the right people." He said sheepishly. "I'm sorry. I thought..."

"It's okay. Thanks anyway." I said.

Eyewitnesses aren't always reliable, but again, any lead was better than nothing. Plus, it got us out of the office. Getting out and doing some digging made me feel less helpless.

Terry and I turned back toward our car but didn't get in. I scanned the area once more, thinking it wouldn't hurt for us to look around. I suggested it to Terry.

"Yeah, good idea." He said. "Should we split up? Cover more buildings."

"Yes. I'll take that side; you take this side."

I jogged across the street. The first building was abandoned, so I checked the door. Locked. I walked around the exterior, trying each window and peeking in. It looked empty, not even leftover furniture or boxes.

I checked the next and so on until I'd talked to everyone in the businesses or checked each abandoned building. I met up with Terry at the end of this street.

"Nothing on my side. I guess the same for you?" He said when we reached each other.

"Yep, nothing. I talked to a few people, but nobody had any information."

"Same."

"This was a bust," I said.

"Should we look at another street before heading back?"

"Couldn't hurt."

We made our way over to the next block and did the same routine. Again, some were vacant while others were still in use. I was able to talk to a few people.

"Yeah, I saw a van around here recently. They were randomly driving around." One guy told me. "A man and woman inside."

"This woman?" I held up the picture.

"Nah, an older woman with light-colored hair. Big guy in the front seat."

He must have seen the same van as Jude, so this was a bust too. Most likely someone lost on their way to the airport.

"Okay, well, thanks."

Two more vacant buildings. The third was empty, but the door was ajar. I looked across the street for Terry but didn't see him. He must be talking to someone in one of the shops.

I hesitated a moment before pushing the door the rest of the way open. "Hello?"

Nothing. I stepped in, pulling out my cell phone and turning on the flashlight app. I wish I had thought to bring a real flashlight from the car.

The first room I entered looked like it had once been a waiting room or lobby of sorts. There were a few chairs and a side table with a few dusty magazines on it. There were two doors from here. One that went straight ahead, which looked like it went back to the warehouse part of the building, and one to my right.

I took the one to the right. The door was stuck but not locked. I pushed it open to reveal a junky office. There were boxes full of files. The desk was turned on its side, and there were several mismatched chairs. Nothing else of interest here.

I then headed toward the warehouse. This door was wide open, but it was pitch black. There were no windows in this part of the building. I hesitated to walk more than a step or two inside because it was difficult to see. I aimed my weak cell phone light around the room. It was generally vacant with a few empty shelves, some trash, and various litter as if people were squatting in here.

I needed to go back for a real flashlight, but I didn't think this was it. I turned to leave just as Terry came in.

"Anything?" He asked.

"Nah. Can't see well, though." I said. "You don't happen to have a flashlight on you, do you?"

He pulled out a penlight from his back pocket, one of those amazingly bright kinds. "Always." He handed it over.

"Ah, much better," I said.

I shined the light around the room and was able to walk a few extra steps in, but sadly nothing here.

"Dang, nothing. I'd hoped for something, some clue." I said.

"Me too. The guys across said only a white van, but nothing else of interest. They didn't even see who was in it, just a van." Terry gestured over his shoulder.

"I guess this was a wild goose chase."

"Yep."

We went back to our car and back to the station. We'd have to hope this guy made a mistake soon.

Chapter Five

Today Janie was taking the baby to her own house because we had a lot going on with the construction of the new deck. When Oakley was awake, she cried at the noise.

Then we also had interviews set up for our new opening act. Technically, we didn't need that extra time to research stories any longer, but we wanted to keep the show the same. No reason to change the format and cause suspicion.

First up this morning was the one we were most looking forward to and our first choice, Fabio. I'd only seen some YouTube clips of him, but he had a good presence and great humor.

When he arrived, Micah greeted him at the door. Micah had done all the screening and setting up the interviews.

"Hey, man. Glad you could make it. Come in, come in." He held the door open for Fabio. "Let me help you with your trunk."

"Thanks, Micah."

"So, Fabio, this is my boss Joanna and co-worker Tessa."

He looked like a typical middle-aged man. A bit on the short side, a bit overweight. Dark hair and a bit of stubble on his face. He smiled at me with wide, crazy eyes. I got that from fans from time to time. A little too excited, nervous, or some overreacted by crying.

"Nice to meet you, Fabio." I put my hand out to shake his.

He grabbed it with both hands and pumped it way too eagerly, for far too long. I smiled through the entire encounter and fought the urge to yank my hand back.

"Oh, I'm so thrilled to meet you! So thrilled. I've been a huge fan forever." Fabio gushed as he grasped my hand as if it was a lifeline. "I've seen several of your shows and have your book, t-shirts, key chains, all of it."

Yep, this guy was a little too enthusiastic. It was almost to the point of creepy, but I was going to brush it off as his excitement and nervousness for the interview.

"Great. Let's go into the living room. We cleared some space for you to show us a few tricks."

We all went into the other room. He got set up while giving us a rundown of his tricks and how he expected his act to go.

"My first trick will be a card trick, and I'll need a volunteer. Joanna, would you like to help me with this?" He beamed.

"Sure."

He had me pick a card before he shuffled it back in and then went through the various steps. I thought it was going to be the typical one that ends with him showing me my card. In a way, it was, but he surprised me with his use of humor and distraction to reveal the card pulled from my own pocket.

His next trick was juggling with magic incorporated. He'd produce various objects from thin air, and he again used humorous banter to distract us. One more close-up magic trick after and his audition part was over. Time for questions.

"You understand that there is a lot of travel involved. Is that something you could do for a month or more at a time?" I asked.

"Yes, I'm not married, no other commitments. Well, except my mom, but she'll be fine. I'll need to give notice at my current job, or actually jobs. I do a few odd jobs."

"Oh, okay, great. And you have enough tricks to fill the time slot? You would get forty minutes."

"Yes, that was only a sampling of what I can do. I currently do a gig at Barkers on the weekends, and it's roughly thirty minutes. I can easily stretch it to fill the time with another trick or two."

"That answers all my questions. Tessa? Micah? Y'all have questions?"

"None from me, boss." Micah said. "I got to ask all mine during my screening."

"None from me either," Tessa added.

"Do you have any questions for us?" I gestured to Fabio.

"How soon do you think you'll have a decision?"

"As Micah told you on the phone, we are looking at three of you. You're the first we've seen. We have one tomorrow and our last one on Thursday. We'll make a decision after that."

"So, by the end of the week?"

"Yes, definitely."

"Great. I hope they aren't as good as me." He laughed. "But seriously, I really appreciate the opportunity."

He did the over-shaking of my hand thing again. I just smiled politely until it was over.

"Thank you for coming, and again, Micah will let you know our decision."

Micah walked him out. Tessa and I started pushing the furniture back into place.

"So whatcha think, Boss?" Micah asked when he came back into the room.

"Not bad. He had a good way of carrying himself, and his humor was entertaining." I paused. "But did you think he was a little too much?"

"What do you mean?" Micah asked.

"The way he wouldn't let go of her hand for one," Tessa commented.

"Yeah, that. It was almost creepy." I said.

"Ah, well, I'm sure it was just nerves. He's a nice guy. Josh and I have gone to Barkers and caught his act a few times."

"Yeah, that makes sense, I guess." I wasn't entirely sure, but Micah had spent more time with him, so I was going to trust his judgment.

We got back to our daily tasks. I had clients to meet with, and my assistants made sure all things Medium with a Heart ran smoothly.

At the end of the day, Janie brought Oakley back. I had definitely missed having her in the house, so the end-of-the-day reunion was sweet.

"Did y'all have a good day?"

"We did. She's getting good at rolling over, and she enjoyed seeing Buttercup. I think she'd love for you to get a dog." Janie teased.

"Ha, that's just what I need."

With all the traveling I did, I wasn't even sure how the baby would fit in, but at least I could take her with me. A dog would have to be boarded while I was out of town, so I didn't see that happening until I stopped doing tours.

After Janie left, Oakley and I got reconnected. She giggled and babbled at me. She was beginning to make different little sounds. It was so fun to hear her find her voice.

"You are going to be quite a talker when you find your voice."

My phone rang. I checked the display. Clint.

"Hello," I said.

"Hey, Jo."

"Hey. How are you?"

"Good, good." He answered. "So, I was wondering if we could go out again? I would love a do-over on our last date."

"I would like that too," I said.

"Friday night?"

"Yes, that works, and I'll ask Audrey to watch Oakley for me."

"Oh, you don't have to."

"No, it's fine. Audrey has been begging to watch her."

"Great, then it's a date."

We talked a few more minutes, ironing out the details, and then the baby started to get fussy. It was time for her bottle, so we said goodbye.

Chapter Six

I had just walked a client out and was checking my emails when an unfamiliar face floated into the office.

"Hi. Joanna, right?" The young lady spirit asked.

"That's right. How can I help you? Are you with the Browns?" They were my next appointment.

"Um, no. My name is Victoria Sellers."

A light bulb went off in my head. She was the missing teacher that I'd seen all over the news and online. Sadly, it didn't look as if she would be rescued, but there would be more of a recovery.

"Victoria Sellers. Oh, wow, how can I help you?"

"I need your help in finding my body. I can tell you where it is, and you can help the police find it. Maybe?"

"Yes, definitely. What can you tell me?"

"So that's the thing. It's fuzzy."

"Fuzzy, how?" How could she not know where her body is? Wouldn't she have seen it when she left it?

"My soul didn't become, I don't know, alive or aware of things until I was away from it." She paused. "I know it sounds crazy, but I kind of know where to find it."

"So, where is it?"

"Near the airport. There is an old hangar or building, but I don't know exactly which one. Just the general area."

"Okay, well, we can work with that. I'll call the police to report it." I picked up my phone.

"Wait. Should we go look first? I think we could find the exact place," she said.

"What? No, why would I do that?"

"I hate to send the police on a wild goose chase."

"I guess that makes sense." I stared at her for a moment, trying to weigh my options. Janie had Oakley over at her house. It was the middle of the day, plus I only had one more appointment.

"Please, I know my family just wants me found."

No, it didn't make sense at all, so why was I even considering doing it? I thought of everything that could go wrong with this plan, including a stern lecture from Clint on how I should call him first.

"I really should call the police to report it."

"I know what I'm asking is crazy, and yes, the right thing to do is call them, but they have been so close to finding me. There were officers at the airport looking the other day." She paused, letting out a sigh. "Please, they need help finding me, and just telling them the airport won't help."

I knew I was going to go. I knew it was stupid and the wrong decision, but I would ask Micah to come with me. That would at least make it less dumb, or at least that's how I was justifying it to myself.

"Okay, fine. I have an appointment shortly, but after that."

She nodded and said she'd hang close by.

My clients came, and we had a good session. They got to share memories and messages of love, all the best parts of my job.

I was riding on that high as I got in my car to make probably one of the dumbest decisions. Why had I agreed to this? At least I'd thought to ask Micah along with me.

"I'm glad you asked me to come along, Boss, but this isn't the best idea, especially if you'd come by yourself. Heck, even with me along, this isn't smart. We should've let Clint know. You know, since it is his case."

"I know. I don't know what I was thinking." I froze when I realized I might offend our guest. "Oh, Victoria, I'm sorry. I know this is important to you, but I need to be safe."

She was hovering along with us in the backseat.

"I understand. I wouldn't ask if I thought there was a better idea."

I bit my tongue because, honestly, the better idea, the best idea, would've been to call the police immediately. My nosy nature and her hopeful expression had me making this stupid drive. I swear I was the cat that they wrote the saying about. Curiosity was going to be my undoing for sure.

But I didn't see the harm in looking. What could go wrong in simply driving around to see if something jogged her memory? It wasn't like I was going to engage with anyone.

It was just a drive, I reminded myself.

I looked over at Micah. I felt safe enough with him here. He was a good friend to come along.

"This is dumb," I muttered.

"Yeah."

"Well, I appreciate it," Victoria said.

We got close to the airport and to the area where the public hangars were. These were privately used and not under TSA control. There were various businesses out here as well. Years ago, I used a body shop out here to repair my car.

But while some were still in use, others looked long abandoned.

"Does anything look familiar?"

"Um, a little. Take a right at the next corner?"

I followed her directions, driving deep into hangars and warehouses. I came to a stop sign and several choices.

"Which way now?" I asked her.

"I'm not sure. This doesn't look right." She turned around to look behind us. "Maybe back this way?"

I turned, and we took a different path. I felt like we were getting all mixed up, and I couldn't remember which roads we'd already driven.

"Are you sure we're in the right area?"

"Yes, yes. This is starting to look right." She moved to float between the front seats. "Oh, yes, over there. That building."

"You're sure?" I'd thought we were looking for an old hangar based on what she had told me, but this was barely a storage shed.

"Yes, that one looks right." Her tone was excited, so I had to believe her.

I parked in front of it. It was quieter in this part of the airport, and I didn't see anyone in this area like what we'd seen in the other sections. If this really was where her body was, I could understand why the Playhouse Killer had picked this spot.

"Should we have a look?" Micah asked.

I hesitated a moment. Getting out meant this wasn't just a drive, but it seemed safe enough. I looked around once, then nodded.

We hopped out and walked to the building.

It was a metal building that looked like it had seen better days. There were a few dingy windows along the top of the walls. The door was slightly ajar, but not enough to see in.

Victoria disappeared into the building without us. She hadn't said a word, so I wasn't sure if we should wait or go in after her. When she didn't return immediately, I decided we should join her to see what was going on. I knew she couldn't be kidnapped or hurt again since she was already dead, but what was holding her up?

I pulled the door open, looking over my shoulder at Micah. "This was such a dumb idea. Why did I do this?"

"You've got a kind heart, Boss." He smiled.

"That makes me immune to danger?" I joked, trying to lighten the mood.

"Probably not."

As our eyes adjusted to the dark shed, it was clear this was where her body was. The smell was indescribable and what I imagined a rotting body smelled like. It was like a mix of decaying cabbage and fish with a bit of something I couldn't quite put my finger on.

Micah and I both gagged.

"I think we've found it."

Victoria appeared with wide eyes. "It's creepy to see myself like that."

"So, I don't need to go further?" The smell was almost unbearable, and I didn't want to see a dead body if I didn't have to.

"No, I think we are good to report this now." She confirmed.

We turned to walk back outside, to the fresh air, but before we could, the door slammed shut. Then there was a metallic sound of the lock engaging. Someone had locked us in.

"What the heck?" Micah exclaimed. He tried the door. "We're locked in."

He started banging and yelling.

"Who would do that?"

Victoria flew through the wall, returning a moment later. "I saw a dark green sedan, but I couldn't catch up to it."

"Great," I said, looking around and trying not to inhale too much.

I pulled out my cell phone. "Almost no signal."

"Me too, Boss," Micah said, looking at his.

We both tried to make calls. I reached Clint.

"Hello." He said.

"Clint, hey."

"Jo, are you there? You're breaking up."

"I need help." I moved closer to the door, trying to get a better signal and as far from the smell as possible.

"I can barely hear you. Did you say you need help?"

"Yes," I shouted into the phone.

"Where are you? In a cave?"

"Near the airport with a dead body."

"Shit, Joanna, I really hope I heard you wrong."

"If you heard me say a dead body, you heard right."

"How do you do this to yourself? I'm on my way." He said. "Where are you exactly?"

I told him the best I could and said my car was outside. I had to keep repeating because the signal wasn't strong, but I think he got enough. I hoped my car being outside would help him find me.

"And, Clint, please hurry. This stinks to high hell."

An hour later, I was finally breathing fresh air and thankful I hadn't lost my lunch in the process.

"What the hell were you thinking, Jo? Coming here instead of calling the police?" Clint lectured. Though his words were stern, his tone was softer. "This was dangerous, and she was already dead, so it wasn't like you could help her."

"But that's the point. She was dead and asked me to find her body. She asked if we could make sure before sending y'all over, saying y'all had already looked around but hadn't found her. I could help, and I did."

"Yeah, but at what cost." He rubbed his face. "Look, it doesn't work that way. It's our job to look, to find. It was dumb." He folded his arms and stared at me. "You could have been hurt too."

"I'm sorry. I knew it was stupid, and I knew better. I just... I'm sorry."

"Please, try to stay out of trouble."

"I'll try, but you did get me involved in this." I pointed out.

"I simply asked if you could talk to some of the victims. Not go chasing after bodies."

"I know, and I did. This victim asked for my help, and I thought I could give it. It's just who I am."

He sighed and looked over at some of the other officers that had joined. They had to do the full evidence gathering and investigation.

I wasn't entirely sorry for what I'd done because we did find her body. That was the goal, and now her family could have closure. I didn't admit that to Clint, though.

"I am sorry about this. I knew better, but she wanted help, and I let my nosiness get me in trouble again. I didn't think there was any danger in looking. I didn't know we would get locked in."

"So, you didn't see anyone follow you? You've had enough experience to know."

"I should have, but I was too busy following her directions."

"Please, please promise me you will call me next time." He paused. "What am I saying? Let's not hope for a next time."

"Agreed."

"Plus, if you get yourself in trouble, I won't get that second date." He winked.

"Ha, ha, detective."

Micah and I gave statements before being cleared to go, just as the media was pulling up. Good timing. We got out just in time to miss out on that nightmare.

We drove back in near silence. There wasn't much to say. We'd had a scary and gross experience that would likely haunt us both for a while.

Once home, I thanked him for being with me and apologized again for getting him into trouble.

"Boss, I'll be by your side through thick and thin." He hugged me and kissed the top of my head. "You're one of my best friends."

"Awe, you're one of my best friends too. Love you, Micah."

"Love you too."

With that, he left. Janie was on her way with Oakley now, so I went to shower and change out of these stinky clothes. I doubted I would ever get the smell of dead body out of my nasal passages.

I still had no regrets, and I'd probably do it all over again if another victim asked me. That was just how I was. Caring and helpful, but nosy to a fault. Deadly combo.

Clint had no idea that when he asked me for help on this case, I was going to give it my all. Or did he? Is that why they asked me? I may never know.

Chapter Seven

~Joanna~

The week went by fast. Donovan had made a lot of progress on the deck. I was thrilled with the quality of his work, so I planned to ask him about helping with the garage storage.

We also decided on our opening act. The next two performers had been good, but we selected Fabio. Despite his over-enthusiasm at meeting me, he genuinely was the best and seemed like he would fit well with our team. Micah called to tell him. He accepted immediately.

With that settled and the workweek complete, it was the day of my second date with Clint. I got Oakley all bundled up, bag packed, and headed over to my sister's house. Audrey had been thrilled with the idea of watching her.

I pulled up at her house, and she came running out.

"Give me my beautiful niece." She took Oakley's car seat from me. "Let's get you inside, little one. You have two excited cousins ready to see you."

I was forgotten, but I didn't mind. I was glad my family had accepted Oakley as if she was my own biological child. It had been something I'd worried about. I grabbed her bag and followed them into the house.

When I stepped in, Harris and Dylan were gushing over her. Harris was five and Dylan was two. Both were thrilled when they first learned about having a baby cousin.

I'd actually been worried they might have some jealousy about no longer being the only grandchildren. However, we'd gotten them cousin shirts and made a big deal about their new role.

My main concern with all of this was the speed at which I'd adopted. Normally, people planned for a baby, whether biological or adopted. I was kidnapped and then offered the kidnapper's baby. My life was weird, but it worked out well for both Oakley and me.

"Hi, baby. Hi. I'm your cousin Harris."

"I Dylan, baby."

Oakley blinked at them. She had been asleep for the drive over. She scanned their faces as she woke up a bit and soon was smiling and cooing at them.

"She likes me." Harris was thrilled.

Dylan clapped and squealed.

"Let me get you out of here." Audrey unbuckled her from the seat. "There you go."

Oakley blinked at her a few times, and her cherub face lit up, and she squealed.

"Awe, we know I'm your favorite person." Audrey gushed over her niece.

"Okay, so she got a new diaper before heading over. She shouldn't need to eat again for about an hour, and I should be back around ten? Maybe." I looked at my daughter, trying to remember everything. "Oh, and she has spare clothes, blankets, and diapers, etc. in the bag."

"Don't worry, mama. I do have experience. We'll be fine."

"I know. I know. This is still all new to me."

"I understand, but don't worry. The boys and I can handle this. Right, boys?"

"Right, mommy!"

I said my goodbyes and gave Oakley one more kiss before heading out to meet Clint.

He picked me up at my sister's house. When I climbed into his truck, I noticed the flowers in the backseat.

"Are those for me?"

"They are." He smiled and handed them over. "I figured you could leave them at your sister's since we're going to be out for a while."

"That's sweet. Thank you." I inhaled the sweet scent. "Let me run these back in."

I hurried back to Audrey's door. She answered with a knowing grin.

"Someone's got an admirer."

"Shut up." I handed her the flowers. "Can you put these in water for me?"

"Of course. Now go have fun."

Back in the truck, Clint had the radio playing softly.

"So where are we headed?" I asked.

"Barkers. It's a comedy and magic club. Fabio is performing tonight, actually. Thought it might be fun to see his full act since y'all hired him."

"Oh, that's a great idea. I've heard of that place but never been."

"I've been a few times. Good food, good entertainment."

We chatted easily on the drive. The getting-to-know-you phase was still in full swing, and I found myself enjoying learning about him.

"I'm not sure how late we will be. The show starts at seven, so I should be back, what? No later than nine or ten?" I looked at Clint for reassurance. He nodded his agreement.

We pulled up to Barkers. I'd never been here before, but I'd heard it was an interesting place. We'd eat dinner, and then starting at seven, there would be stand-up comedians and magicians until Fabio's show. He was the headliner.

We got seated quickly and not far from the stage. I looked around at the quirky, unique décor. It looked like it had been decorated in the styling of an old circus sideshow, the kind that had the world's strongest man or the bearded lady.

Vintage circus posters hung in heavy wood and gold-trimmed frames, along with funhouse mirrors and replica props they might use. Framing the stage were thick purple velvet curtains tied back with gold tassels. The staff were dressed in various circus costumes, and all played the part well.

"This is an interesting place," I said as I picked up my menu.

"Very interesting."

We read over the menus, made our selections, and then placed our order with the waitress. She left some freshly baked bread and cinnamon butter. I had a weakness for warm bread, and all the best places served it, or at least in my opinion.

We each ate a slice of bread and chatted casually while we waited for our meals. We were still in the fun getting-to-know-you stage, so there were still a lot of childhood stories or "this one time in college" moments to share.

Once we had eaten dinner and ordered a cocktail, it was time for the first performer to take the stage. We laughed along with the rest of the audience as the comedian told his tale of growing up in Creekview. It was funny because it was so relatable.

Another comedian took the stage, followed by a magician. This one wasn't quite as good as Fabio. He'd applied for the job but hadn't made it past the review stage. Still, he was entertaining but couldn't have held the stage for a full forty minutes as needed for our shows.

Finally, it was time for the main event, Fabio. I couldn't wait to see his full act in person.

He took the stage in full costume and tons of props. He started his act with some juggling, much like he'd done in my living room, but on a grander scale by getting a few people close to the stage involved. He made things "appear" on their tables and asked them to throw it to him.

After that, he did a card trick. He asked the audience to shout out numbers, and he wrote a few on one of the cards. He then shuffled and flipped and shuffled some more. He did some other fancy finger work until he produced the card with the writing on it.

"Next up... wait a minute, folks. Do we have a celebrity in the house?" His eyes were on me. "It's Creekview's very own Joanna the Medium with a Heart."

Oh crap, I thought as all eyes turned to me, and a murmur started in the crowd. I put on my best stage smile and stood waving around the room. There were cheers, and a little crying started. That always happened. Grief was a weird thing bringing out a range of emotions.

"Should I bring her up on stage?" Fabio asked the eager audience.

The crowd went crazy. I tried to blow it off, but I gave in to the fans. I could feel my stage persona coming to the surface as I walked to join him.

"Thank you, all. I don't want to take away from the wonderful performers we have had here tonight." I said into the microphone that an employee handed me as I walked onto the stage. "Haven't they all been great? Let's give them all a round of applause."

The audience did just that, clapping and cheering, but then people started shouting for me to reach their loved ones.

"I want to speak to my mother. Her name's Tonia." One voice said.

"My father, Michael, would have been 100 today. Can you connect with him?"

"My great-aunt..."

"My sister..."

I heard so many voices. It was starting to become overwhelming. And if the living voices weren't bad enough, then the dead ones began in reply to some of the requests. I couldn't do this. My senses were overloaded, and the room started to spin.

"I'm sorry, everyone. That's not why I'm here." I looked over at Fabio and then down to Clint. "Let me give the stage back to Fabio."

Fabio mouthed he was sorry and started addressing the crowd, but I couldn't hear him over all the voices.

I swiftly walked off the stage, handing the mic back to the stagehand, and tried to make my way back to our table. However, people were starting to get up and mob me. Crowding around to the point I couldn't see Clint any longer.

"Clint?" I called out, then tried to push my way through the people. "I'm sorry, please, let me get back to my table."

I tried asking for people to let me by. I couldn't see anything above the crush of people. This had never happened before.

"Step back." I heard Clint's voice boom over the crowd, but people didn't move much.

We both kept working through the crowd to get to the other person. Relief filled my body when I finally saw his face. He grabbed me around the waist and guided me toward the door.

The club security guard also got to us and was able to hold back the mob to escort us to the door.

I was so thankful when we finally made it out and were safely back in his truck. With the crowd outside of it, I could breathe.

"Wow, that was crazy." He said, handing me my purse. "You okay?"

"Yes, yes. Thanks. I've never had that happen before."

"I'm glad I was with you."

"Me too. I'm sorry about your evening. I know you wanted to see Fabio's show."

"Don't worry about it. I've seen it before, and your safety is more important."

I smiled at him. He really was a good guy.

We sat in his truck for a moment, letting the adrenaline settle.

"So, what now?" I asked.

"I could take you home, or we could go somewhere quieter?"

"Quieter sounds nice."

We ended up at a small coffee shop that was open late. We talked for another hour, and by the time he dropped me off at my sister's to get Oakley, it was close to eleven.

"I had a good time tonight, despite the chaos," I said.

"Me too. We should do it again sometime. Maybe somewhere without an audience."

I laughed. "Deal."

Audrey was half asleep on the couch when I came in to get Oakley.

"Hey, how'd it go?" She yawned.

"Good. Interesting. I'll tell you about it later."

"She was an angel." Audrey nodded toward the baby sleeping in the portable crib.

I carefully gathered up my daughter and her things, thanked my sister, and headed home.

When I pulled into my driveway, something felt off. I couldn't put my finger on it at first. It wasn't until I got closer to the front door that I saw it.

Spray-painted across my beautiful front door in bright red letters was one word: BITCH.

My heart dropped to my stomach. Who would do this? And why?

I stood there staring at it, Oakley sleeping peacefully in her car seat, completely unaware that someone had targeted our home.

I pulled out my phone and called Clint.

"Hey, everything okay?" He answered on the second ring.

"Someone vandalized my house. They spray-painted 'bitch' on my front door."

"What? I'm on my way. Don't go inside until I get there."

"Okay."

I sat in my car with the doors locked, watching my house and waiting for Clint. The word glared at me from across the yard, angry and red.

Who would do this? Was it random? Or was someone targeting me specifically?

By the time Clint arrived, my mind had run through a dozen possibilities, each one worse than the last.

He checked the perimeter of the house while I waited in the car. When he gave the all-clear, I carried Oakley inside while he took pictures of the door.

"Any ideas who might have done this?" He asked once we were inside.

"None. I mean, I've had unhappy clients before, but nothing like this."

"What about the serial killer case? You've been helping us. Someone could know."

The thought sent a chill down my spine. "You think it's connected?"

"I don't know, but we can't rule it out."

He stayed until I felt safe enough for him to leave, promising to have a patrol car drive by regularly through the night.

After he left, I double-checked all the locks and the security system before finally settling into bed with Oakley in her bassinet beside me.

Sleep didn't come easily that night. Every creak of the house had me on edge. Someone knew where I lived. Someone was angry enough to vandalize my home.

And I had no idea who.

Chapter Eight

I woke up the next day in a bed I was becoming way too familiar with. I was thankful to my sister and brother-in-law for letting me stay.

Even more thankful that they still had some baby supplies left from their boys, like a portable crib for Oakley. It had made staying over much more comfortable for the two of us.

"Good morning, Oaky-girl. Did you sleep well?"

She smiled and cooed her reply. I changed her diaper, and then we headed to the kitchen, so I could fix her a bottle.

"Auntie Jo." Harris ran to me and wrapped his arms around me. "I'm so happy to see you. We had so much fun with Cousin Oakley last night. She laughed at all my jokes. Nobody ever laughs that much at my jokes."

"I laugh at your jokes, at least the first twenty times." Audrey teased him. "Coffee, sis?"

"Yes, please." I started to fix Oakley's bottle. I had gotten good at doing things one-handed. A skill I never knew I would need.

Audrey set the steaming mug in front of me. "So, rough night, huh? Any ideas?"

"None. Clint and Terry asked for help on a case, but I'm not even doing any active investigating right now, not like last time with Jeremy. I keep wondering if it's a random stalker, but why?"

"That's scary."

"Don't tell mom." I snapped quickly.

"Do I look stupid?"

We laughed. We both knew we'd never share anything like this with our mom, but we always reminded the other.

"And then I didn't tell you yet, but Micah and I got trapped in an abandoned building with a dead body."

"What?" She gasped.

"Yeah. So that teacher that's been missing, she came to see me and asked me to find her body." I took a sip of coffee and judged her facial expression to see if she was upset, but she didn't look like it yet. "While I knew better than to go, I did it anyway."

"Of course, you did. Nosy to a fault but kindhearted. Like when we were kids, and you tried to help Grams and Uncle Peter solve his murder."

"Yeah, but I knew it was stupid, then and now. Anyway, we get over there, find the right building, and before we could get out of the building, someone locked us in."

"Joanna, I can't believe it." She scolded. "No ideas who?"

"Nope. Not a clue. Like I said, I've only talked to dead people so far. Only Clint, Terry, Micah, and now you are the only ones who even know about this. Tessa doesn't even know yet that I'm doing this."

She looked at Oakley in my arms. "You need to be careful, not just for you, but for her."

"I know."

I finished feeding Oakley and drank my coffee while enjoying time with my sister and her family. Unfortunately, I had a lot to deal with today. I hoped I could get someone to clean my door, and I needed to figure out how to fix the security alarm.

"I can fix your alarm for you, Jo." Stan offered. He's the one that had installed it.

"Thanks, that would be a huge help," I said.

"I'll come over later and get you fixed up."

I gathered our things, loaded the baby into the car, and told Audrey we would be back if I couldn't get the alarm fixed today. I sent off a text to Clint as he had asked me to. He replied that he'd meet us there.

I drove home looking for any followers. For a few streets, there was a dark green sedan behind me, then a red SUV for a couple more, but those were the only ones that seemed suspicious.

Honestly, they never got close or gave any real indication they were following me, other than going in the same direction for more than two streets. I had become so paranoid.

I also ran through the list of what-ifs. What if someone were out to get me again? What if I put the baby in danger? What if I couldn't protect her? Maybe I should have left her at Audrey's until I assessed the situation.

We pulled up in front of our house, and I saw Clint's truck at the curb. I let out my breath. I didn't realize I was holding it.

I got parked, just as he came around the corner from the backyard. I smiled at the sight of him. He was a handsome man with his slight swagger and messy bedhead styled hair.

"Good morning, ladies." He waved a finger at Oakley. "I was doing a quick perimeter check. I couldn't have y'all coming home to any issues."

"Thanks. I appreciate that."

He helped me get our bags and the baby into the house. It felt so good to be home. I hated being run out of here so often. I got the baby settled into her pack-n-play with some toys while Clint did an internal check of the house.

I messaged Micah, Tessa, and Janie about the graffiti on the door, so they wouldn't be caught off guard. They all replied quickly. I tried to blow it off as nothing, but internally I was freaking out.

We might need to reschedule clients if I wasn't able to get it cleaned up. I hated it when I had to change my schedule. I was always booked. Any bump in it made it difficult to fit those customers in on another day.

"Everything inside looks good," Clint said, coming back into the living room.

"Great."

"Do you want me to stay until someone else gets here?"

"I think I'll be okay. I really appreciate your coming over, though. It means a lot."

"Of course. I want you to be safe."

He wrapped his arms around me, making me feel so safe. This was something I didn't even know I was missing, but here it was.

"I'll call you later." He kissed me softly.

I think I mumbled something, but his lips left me speechless.

I watched him as he drove off. About the time Clint's truck disappeared, Donovan pulled up. He had a little bit of work to do on my deck.

"Oh, no. Joanna, what happened to your door?"

"Vandal." I shrugged, and then a thought struck me. "Oh, hey, could you help me clean it up? Do you do that?"

"Definitely. I can get started right now." He opened the back of his van and started digging around. "What time is your first client?"

"At ten."

"Okay, so we have a bit of time for me to get this more presentable for you."

"If you could, that would be amazing. I thought I might have to cancel."

"I'll make sure you don't have to do that." He winked.

He started pulling out tools, a couple of cans of what looked to be paint, and then set up a couple of sawhorses. I excused myself back into the house.

As I stepped in, my phone rang. It was my mom. Great. What had Marcy told her now? Marcy Dalton was my mom's best friend and, unfortunately for me, lived on my street. I hadn't realized she lived here until after I'd fallen in love with and bought the house.

"Hi, mom."

"Joanna Lynn, what is going on over there? Marcy Dalton called me. She said there was a bad word painted on your door."

Darn it, Marcy. I should probably consider moving.

"It's nothing. Just a vandal or something."

"Is my sweet granddaughter in danger? Bad enough my daughter talking to dead people and getting kidnapped all the time."

"One time, mom. It was one time."

"You should consider going back to accounting now that you have a baby to think about."

"We're fine. She's safe."

There was murmuring on the other end of the phone.

"Hello?" my dad said.

I guess mom passed the phone to my dad. She must have a "headache." I was always the cause of her illnesses.

"Hi, dad."

"Oh, hi, Jo. How's it going? What did you do to your mom now?" He said it teasingly. He knew how she was, and this was more of a her issue than a me issue.

"Oh, you know, me being me."

"Well, I better check on her. Be safe and kiss my sweet Oakley for me."

"I will. Love you, dad."

An hour later, Janie and Tessa were here. Tessa was reading me the riot act. Another lecture this morning. What a day.

"What have you gotten yourself into now?" Her arms crossed.

"I have no idea."

"This isn't normal, Jo." Tessa tapped her foot.

"Yeah, I know, and this time I haven't even actively investigated anything. Three spirits talked to me, but nobody else knows about them. People might know I found Victoria's body, but it wasn't like I was interviewed by the media and wasn't named as the person who found her."

"So, are we thinking a crazed fan then, not related to this case?"

"Maybe. Or did I give someone a bad reading? I don't remember anyone being unhappy, except maybe that widow looking for her husband's banking information." I said.

"Yeah, I remember she wasn't super happy, but that was back in the faking it days, and it was a long time ago."

"I don't think I'll figure it out, but I sure hope it was just a random thing."

Donovan stuck his head in. "Joanna, I think I'm done with the door. Would you like to have a look before I hang it?"

"Wow, that was fast."

It had only been an hour. My first client wasn't due for another hour, so he definitely more than beat the deadline.

I followed him, and Tessa joined us.

"Oh, wow, this looks so much better."

He'd painted my door a deep navy-blue color. I would have never thought to do that, but it was necessary to hide the word.

"I sanded it down as much as I could to get the spray paint off and then since I had to paint it anyway, I thought this color would look good." He smiled at me. "So, you like it?"

"Very much. It looks so good."

"It's going to still be wet for a bit and will be tacky to the touch for a while, so I'll post a sign."

"Okay," I turned to Tessa. "Maybe you and Micah can take turns meeting and escorting the clients in, so they don't touch it?"

"Not a problem."

"Great. I'll start hanging the door and post a sign, then get back to work on the deck. I should be done today or tomorrow at the latest."

"Perfect. I appreciate it."

Later, Stan came and fixed the security system, which would help me sleep at night and not have to run back to my sister's.

Thankfully, the rest of the day was fairly uneventful. I hoped it stayed that way. I hated to think something I'd done had put Oakley in danger.

Chapter Nine

~ Stalker ~

She went out with him again. Why? What did she see in him? Seeing them together was frustrating, and I wanted to punch someone.

I paced in my room, kicking at stray clothing that littered the floor, and then threw my shoe at the wall.

Even a day later, I was still mad, but I did what I had to do to send a message. She should be with me, but I didn't know how to tell her. With all the people always around, she hadn't paid much attention to me yet.

Not a surprise, though. I'd spent my whole life blending in. I didn't know how to stand out.

With my mother's many boyfriends, I tried to be invisible, or else they would torture me, beating me and molesting me. She often joined in the torture.

Life was frustrating, and my anger boiled over. I took it out on wild animals or neighborhood cats. I had to get the pain out by causing pain. I couldn't hurt my mother or the boyfriends, but I hurt anyone else and everything else I could get my hands on.

With Joanna, it would be different. I would be so gentle. I would make her fall in love with me. I just had to get her to notice me, and not only as some guy but as a man she could love. The man she deserves. Not that boring detective.

I had to make a bold move, but what would I do? I had a few ideas. It was just going to take time and trial and error to find the one that would work.

At least I'd get to see her, even for only a moment here or there. She didn't know that I had feelings for her. I didn't know how to tell her, but I'd do whatever it takes to be near her.

The teacher had at least fed my need for Joanna. It put out the fire of frustrations deep inside me. I tried to fight the demons as long as possible, but I always gave in to the urges.

"Son! Son, where are you?" came the voice of my now elderly mother.

"I'm in here, mother," I yelled out from my room.

"I need you." She screeched. The sound was like nails on a chalkboard.

She was disabled, though I suspected it was mostly due to her own laziness, and it had taken a toll on her body. Due to this, she tired quickly, had various pains, and she didn't go out much. It forced me into the role of her nurse and caregiver. I hated it and hated her.

Some days, I wish she would just die already!

The thought of it had me shaking my head. I didn't mean it. I might kill random people but couldn't imagine doing that to her, even if I fantasized about it often and knew exactly how to do it to make it appear to be an accident. Specifically, a drug overdose.

She was on so many that it wouldn't be that far-fetched. Perhaps I gave her a dose. Later she forgot taking the first dose and takes another. People would believe that, or at least anyone that knew her. She was forgetful at times and depended on me for most everything.

Plus, it was a fight we had almost daily. She'd argue she needed to take her medicine. I'd argue she had taken it or maybe it wasn't time. I had a journal and a daily pill organizer. I was on top of it.

If I ever changed my mind about taking care of her, I would simply not fight with her and give her the pills. I knew the right combo to make it deadly.

As my mother's nurse, I'd learned how to give her shots and how to dose it. I'd taken a few classes that were offered at the hospital to help caregivers. Not many people knew about that, but it helped with capturing my victims.

I let out a laugh. Victims. They only knew of some of them. There were more. I knew better than to kill all my targets in Creekview. That was a sure way to get caught. I couldn't get seen, not ever.

For now, I let my mom live, but she'd made my life hell since my birth, all because I wasn't born a girl. She'd wanted a daughter and made sure I heard about it almost every day of my life.

That's not what moms are supposed to do. Aren't they supposed to be happy with the child they have? She never was.

"Son!" she yelled out. "I need you."

Cringing when I heard the word son. It was intended derogatory.

I looked around my room, sighed, and then went to see what this witch wanted from me now. I'd feed my demons later.

Chapter Ten

~Clint~

Looking over my notes for the serial killer case, it was the toughest one I'd worked. Most cases were fairly clear cut, or so I thought. The Landon case hadn't been as apparent as it had first appeared. There had to be some clue in here that I'd missed like in that case.

Maybe it was how the ladies connected to each other? But in reviewing, nothing jumped out at me. They all had different types of jobs, different circles of friends, and none had a family relation. The only thing that appeared similar was their physical appearance.

The similarities between the victims and Joanna had me worried about her, even if it was likely a coincidence. To date, there was no reason to suspect this had anything to do with her.

Though she had some graffiti on her door, again, no evidence it was related. It could be a disgruntled fan or neighbor.

Then again, being locked in that abandoned building with one of the dead victims was harder to shake off as nothing. Still, no clue who it was or why.

Had it been someone nearby that hadn't realized they were inside? I had my doubts about that, but since there had been no direct threats made to her or Micah, there was no reason for her and Micah to be targeted this way. I was dumbfounded.

I started looking at the locations each victim had been found at. Was there a significance there? With the Landon case, all of the murders happened at the lab using the same type of chemical mix. In this case, nothing jumped out at me as connecting the locations, such as owned by the same company or landlord.

Nor was there a pattern to the locations, like close to the airport or close to downtown. Nothing like that. They weren't even always close to where the victim was taken.

They were abandoned buildings and one abandoned house. He had used a few sites more than once but in different parts of the building from the others.

This is why the media had nicknamed him the Playhouse Killer because he used these vacant places and the way he tortured them, almost toying with them. It was gruesome. I was so ready to end this guy's reign.

He understood how to cover his tracks well and had avoided being caught on security cameras, which were everywhere nowadays. It blew my mind how he was able to go unseen. Not even a shadow.

I didn't believe in such things, but that didn't mean my mind didn't think it. Was this guy a ghost? No fingerprints, no DNA other than that of the victims, no murder weapon found. Nothing.

I ran my hands through my hair. The only thing I knew for sure, I had to solve this before we lost any more victims to him.

Terry stuck his head in my office and knocked on the wall.

"Victim. Looks like the serial killer again."

"Crap. Where?"

"Empty house on the border of Creekview and Buckston."

This one was on the border of our jurisdiction. Not his usual location. He'd never gone this far out of town before. Well, almost out of town.

On the drive over, Terry asked, "So, any word from Joanna about any victims?"

"Nothing much. She's talked to a couple of them, but they couldn't offer anything concrete."

"How's that even possible? They didn't see him?"

"Apparently not. She said they'd been grabbed from behind and injected with a drug. We know from the autopsies that it's diazepam. If given in the right dose, as you know, it can cause memory loss and unconsciousness, which Jo has noted all the victims seem to have. Just vague memories." I shook my head.

"I hate to admit it, but this guy is good. Almost to the point of disgusting." Terry said. He paused, appearing to be thinking. "So, what's the deal with you two?"

"With me and Joanna? What do you mean?"

"You said y'all went out a few times. Does that mean you're dating now?"

"I don't know. We haven't talked about it, but just casually dating. Getting to know each other a bit." I rubbed the stubble on my face as I thought. "I can't get more serious. You know that."

"I know. But do you have any idea how she feels?" He said. "She has a baby and probably not into something casual."

"True." I had already thought about that. "No, I have no idea what she's thinking."

"Well, you need to figure it out before you waste her time and yours."

"You're right. It's a pattern with me, and I own it."

"Monica was a long time ago, bud."

"Yeah."

Her name still caused a lightning bolt of pain through my heart. I had no idea if that would ever go away. Monica had been the one, and I assumed I was destined to be alone, filling my time with this fling or that one.

And yet there was Joanna Webber. She was the first woman in a while to cause me to pause and think about my feelings. Not only why had I dragged out a break-up, but how I felt about the person.

I liked her and was attracted to her. She was an interesting, beautiful, and caring person. The couple of dates we'd been on had been nice, though slightly awkward as first dates sometimes were.

On our second date, we'd both shared some personal things, but hadn't talked further about what we might be to each other. I got the impression she wasn't in the serious space either, but without talking to her about it, I wouldn't know for sure.

Thankfully, I was saved from thinking further as we arrived at the crime scene. We exited the car, and I took it in fully. It was a residential area on the edge of a business park. The house was older and appeared to have been recently remodeled. This area of town was going through changes as they tried to revitalize it.

Terry and I spoke with the lead on the scene. She filled us in on all the details they had so far.

"Twenty-eight-year-old victim. She'd been reported missing the other night when she didn't make it home after her shift at Leo's. Her car was still there, so she was taken from that area."

"Who found her here?" I asked.

"A real estate agent that was showing the property. She finished her statement, and we've already sent her home."

"Okay, good."

I looked down at the body and the surrounding area, trying to see anything unusual or unique to this murder. While I didn't want another murderer running around, I didn't want yet another Playhouse Killer victim. However, by the looks of the body, it had all the earmarks for the serial killer we'd been chasing.

Damn, I thought.

"And you said she worked at Leo's. Any connection to Hank?" Hank the Hammer was a local entrepreneur that barely toed the line with what is legal. Rumor had it he runs an underground, illegal gambling club and other "business" dealings. He helps us out from time to time, so we mostly looked the other way, but it also meant he had a pulse on what we did. A 'you scratch my back, I scratch yours' kind of thing.

"Yes, and he's been notified and is on his way here."

"Wonderful." I rolled my eyes. That's just what I need right now, to be interrogated by Hank. I had more questions than answers, and he wouldn't like that.

We also had to deal with the media who had just shown up. A uniformed officer had finished setting up the perimeter to keep them back. We had our public relations expert preparing to give a statement.

We spoke with the forensic team, but they said they hadn't found much. This guy had one sloppy scene a few months ago but has been much more careful since. That one print we found hadn't given us enough clues to identify the killer.

They were preparing to take the body when Hank and Al showed up. Al was Hank's right-hand man and was rarely far from his boss's side.

"Hartley. Walden." Hank nodded to us.

"Hank." We nodded back.

"May I see her?"

I hesitated because we usually didn't allow that, especially to non-family members. However, the relationship with Hank was complicated, and it was the same reason he got called when she'd been found.

"Yes, that's fine." I nodded to the coroner's employees that were pushing the body out.

He opened the body bag. Hank and Al looked at her. Tears formed in Hank's eyes. I never thought I would see that, but the man did have a heart, and he genuinely cared about our town.

"That's her. Sweet girl. Too young." He shook his head.

"Can you give us any information on whom she might have been hanging out with? Any new boyfriends or guys hanging around?" I asked.

"She's been hanging with my guy Darius. He's a good guy, and I can give his alibi. He was working with me." Hank looked at Al, who simply nodded. "So, y'all have no leads? Isn't she like the eighth or ninth victim that this bastard has killed?"

"Yes, unfortunately, we don't have much to go on. Except this guy looks to have a type, there aren't many clues. No connection and not much evidence."

"You need to find this guy." Hank pointed a finger at each of us. "Our town's a safe place, and we all work to keep it that way."

"I agree, and we're doing our best. We're just as heartbroken with each victim." Terry said.

"Well, now that my girl here is involved, you know we will be as well. I have ears and eyes in places that y'all don't. I'll help in any way I can."

"We appreciate that, but you know the drill. Don't take the law into your own hands and let us do our job." I said, knowing it would fall on deaf ears, but I had to at least say it out loud.

He nodded his agreement and then turned with Al on his flank. They left as quietly and quickly as they arrived.

We wrapped up and left. I hated that we didn't have more answers. Each time we left these scenes, I thought of the victims' family and friends. Thankfully, it wasn't part of my job to inform the families.

While I was staring down at the recent victim, it made me think of Joanna. I was concerned again for her safety. This had to be the connection between them, the physical looks.

That thought left me a bit shaken because I knew that somewhere in me, I had feelings for Jo and that opened me up to being hurt again, especially if something happened to her. Could I ever recover from two broken hearts?

Despite the potential for heartache, I knew I had to reach out, to know she was safe. I sent her a simple text to say hi. Her reply was instant and put my mind at ease that, at least for the moment, she was okay.

My phone chimed, signaling another text. My heart beat quickened as I thought perhaps another message from Jo, but it was my mom. She had yet another lady for me to date. I rolled my eyes. I may not know how I felt about Jo, but I did know I didn't want to date anyone else. I replied, no, thanks.

Immediately, my phone rang. I flashed the phone display at Terry. "Hello, mom."

"Clint Michael Hartley, what do you mean, no thanks?"

"I'm not interested in dating anyone right now. That's all."

"You're going to die alone, and I'm going to be grand-childless until I die."

"You have grandchildren, mom. Brandy has two kids, and Travis has four."

"You don't have any, and I want more."

"I don't know what to tell you. I'm just not interested."

"Fine. It's probably best you don't have kids. They'll only break your heart like you're breaking mine." She sniffled softly.

"Okay, mom, look," I sighed. She wasn't usually the dramatic type, so I knew this was serious to her. "I'm sort of... I'm sort of seeing someone."

"Oh, Clint, you are?" My mom brightened immediately. "Who is she?"

I thought for a moment. Should I tell her, not tell her? The cat was halfway out of the bag, so to speak. I might as well tell her the whole truth.

"It's Joanna, that medium."

"Oh, I love her! Have you seen her do a live reading? She's so good."

"I haven't."

"You'll have to introduce me. I would love to meet her in person." Mom said.

"Sure, mom."

"I will stop trying to set you up. Oh, I'm so happy."

"Great. Well, Terry and I are pulling up at the station. I gotta go. Love you, mom."

"I love you, Clint."

Once I was off the phone, I looked at Terry. He was holding in laughter.

"Shut up. Don't say it." I warned him.

"I didn't say a word."

Chapter Eleven

Donovan had finished my deck and the front door and had done such a fantastic job that I had him come over to give me a quote for the garage work.

It would be a game-changer for us with selling, shipping, and packing all things Joanna the Medium with a Heart. I was excitedly pacing and watching for him out the window, and when he finally pulled up, I bounced my way outside to meet him.

"Good morning, Donovan."

"Mornin', Ms. Joanna." He grabbed his tool bag as he exited the van.

"I'm so glad you had time to work on another project for me."

"Of course. My pleasure."

We walked to the garage, and I opened the door. I cringed a little when it opened, revealing our hot mess. The cheap plastic shelves we had bought in a pinch were sagging from the weight of the products loaded on them. On the floor, boxes overflowed with all things Joanna the Medium with a Heart, and our makeshift packing area was a crazy mess of trash with wads of discarded tape and paper everywhere.

Half the time, we couldn't find the box cutter or scissors because they would get randomly set down and buried under the mounds of debris.

"Wow." He rubbed his hands through his thin hair. "Okay, okay. No problem. I can work with this."

He listened to my ideas, made some notes, took some measurements, and asked me additional questions. He sketched out a quick plan. Rough as it was, it captured what I wanted.

"Yes, that's exactly what I'm thinking."

"Okay, I think I can do this for $4,500." He cringed as he told me the price. "It could change once I start buying materials and working on it. I'll try to come in at or below the estimate."

If I sold half of what I had in the garage, it would more than pay for the cost, so I didn't bat an eye.

"Great. When can you start?"

"I won't be able to start until next week. I have a couple of other jobs to finish. Is that okay?" He asked.

"Yes, that's fine. Let me know when. While it's a mess, there really is no rush."

I didn't have anywhere to put the products, so they would be moved into my house. I wasn't looking forward to that part of the project, so I didn't mind putting that part off a bit longer.

"Okay, great. I'll let you know." He paused, looking from me to my mess. "I better get to my next job. I'll be back as soon as I can to get to work on this."

"Thanks."

I walked with him to the front yard and watched as he loaded his tool bag into the back. He smiled and waved before driving off.

I continued standing in the driveway, lost in thought as I took in the once beautiful tree-lined street. Since the storm nearly two weeks ago, it had lost some of its charm. The mature trees and character were one of the reasons I fell in love with this house, but some of the trees had lost branches, and one of my favorite trees, several houses down, had uprooted completely. It had since been removed and a sapling planted in its place.

As I stood there, a car passed my house, slowed, then backed up.

"Hey, Joanna!" It was Fabio.

"Hi, Fabio. How are you?" I said, leaning forward to see him better through the car window.

"I'm good." He beamed at me. "I'm so glad you're out here. I was heading to a friend's house nearby to practice, but I wanted to tell you that I really appreciate the opportunity to be your opening act. If I can have half the success that Julio did, I'll be thrilled."

His wild, wide eyes caused a chill to run through my body. Why was I having such an irrational reaction to this guy? He was an amazing magician and seemed like a nice enough guy, just too energetic, which isn't necessarily bad. However, his behavior was almost obsessive and was a bit of a turn-off.

I shook off my attitude and plastered on my best Joanna the Medium smile. "You should get a lot of exposure, that's for sure."

He kept staring at me. I shifted under the weight of his gaze. Thankfully, I heard Oakley on the baby monitor.

"Oh, the baby. I need to go get her. Have a good day, Fabio."

"You too, Joanna." He didn't drive away immediately, but I retreated quickly without looking back.

Throughout the day, I thought of the way he stared at me and his intense eyes. I should be used to rabid fans as I've had a few, but I didn't run into them often. It was only at a show or a reading here or there.

I hoped once the newness of the job offer wore off, he would settle down and be calmer. I did like the guy, at least his short performance for us during the interview and what I viewed of him from YouTube.

I settled in for my long workday and tried to put all thoughts of serial killers and obsessed employees out of my mind. I had more important things to think about, like the Murrays, who were coming to reconnect with their husband and father. There were also the Kings coming to speak to their grandmother. Both families were more important than wasting my brain space on Fabio.

They were successful, fun readings, and the families left happy. That always made my job feel rewarding.

After the last client left and it was just Oakley and me, I spread out a blanket on the floor and put her favorite toys around. I'd just set her down to let her play when there was a knock on the door.

"I swear this house is always busy," I said to the baby, as I scooped her up to answer the door.

Opening it, I found Al and Hank. We'd had dealings before, though I didn't use his "business" services. He'd helped me when I was investigating the Landon Labs murders.

"Hi, Hank. Al." I said.

"Good evening, Ms. Joanna," Hank said. Al only nodded.

"What can I help y'all with this evening?" I juggled the wiggly baby from my shoulder to face forward as she kept trying to see who the voices belonged to.

"Can we come in? It would be best in private, and it looks like the little miss would like to stretch out." He cooed at Oakley, and she grinned.

"Yes, of course, come in." They followed me into the living room. "Can I get y'all a drink?"

"Nothing for me," Hank said, lowering himself into a side chair. "Al?"

He shook his head. I'd never heard Al speak. He stood behind Hank with arms crossed over his chest. Al was not someone I would want to tangle with. He was a tank and a half with muscles on top of muscles. I could see why Hank always had him by his side.

I sat across from Hank with the baby in my lap but facing the strangers as I knew she liked to see people. She was definitely an extrovert like her bio-mom, while her adoptive mother was an introvert.

"First of all, I think it's wonderful what you've done here, taking in the baby. What a sad life she could've had." Hank said with a grin at Oakley.

"Thank you. She's been a blessing."

"The reason I'm here is about Macy. I'm sure you heard about her from Detective Hartley."

"I did, from the news, and I'm very sorry to hear."

"Thank you. She was a sweet girl." He bowed his head before continuing. "Have you had any contact with her, by chance?"

"Not yet. I've talked to three of the serial killer's victims, but they weren't much help."

"In what way?"

"None got a good look at him, though one tried to give me a description. Sadly, it could describe quite a few men in Creekview, even you, but not Al." I eyed Al's huge frame. There was no way you could confuse Al with even the vague description of the killer.

"That's a shame. I was hoping we could have a quick resolution and get this guy."

"Me too," I said.

I think most people would assume that the spirits that visited me knew how they died. Those that had been sick usually did, but those that died accidentally or unexpectedly didn't always remember. Only a few could recall it in detail. Most said it was blurry and had little information about their actual death.

It was worse with these particular victims because they'd all been heavily drugged, plus he had the element of surprise on them. Whatever it was he used, it worked well because they all talked about how hazy things seemed.

"By the way, I noticed you painted your front door. It looks good."

"Oh, thanks. Sadly, it was necessary. I had a bit of graffiti painted on it."

"Oh, what happened?"

"Someone painted the 'B' word on it." I'm not sure why, but I didn't feel comfortable saying the full word to Hank the Hammer. Probably because he reminded me of my old science teacher. It seemed disrespectful.

"While you were home? What about your security cameras?"

"I was out, and whoever did it cut the wires. I guess they knew how to do it because the alarm didn't trigger."

"Al, we'll have to get our men to start watching her again." He said over his shoulder.

Al pulled out a phone, pushed a button, and then stepped down the hallway to talk. Darn, I still didn't get to hear him talk. I could just hear a deep voice.

Hank wiggled his finger at the baby and talked to her. She cooed and smiled at him and tried to grab him.

"She's a sweet baby, Ms. Joanna."

"She really is." I beamed down at my daughter. It made my heart swell that people loved her so much. She was almost like our mascot or a sign of hope of sorts.

Al came back in the room and nodded once to Hank.

"Well, Ms. Joanna, you'll now have round-the-clock eyes on you. If there's any trouble, my guys will be nearby to help."

"Thank you so much. I appreciate this."

We stood, and I walked them out.

I was relieved to be under the protection of Hank the Hammer again. They hadn't saved me from being kidnapped last time, though they'd tried. Still, to have them close was like a second security system.

Chapter Twelve

My parents had agreed to watch Oakley for me tonight, so I could go out with Clint. He'd gotten tickets to the show at Barkers to see Fabio. I'd finally get to see his full show live and in front of an audience.

Seeing the crowd's reaction to him might take away some of the doubts I was having with his slightly unprofessional behavior.

But perhaps in the place he was most comfortable, he would be calmer.

There was a knock at the door.

"Must be Nanny and Grampa," I said to Oakley.

I picked her up and walked to the door. I swung it open to see Clint, not my parents.

"Oh, hi, you're early." I smiled.

"Yeah, sorry, I thought traffic might be heavier, but I got lucky."

"Yeah, it can be a nightmare sometimes." I stepped aside, gesturing for him to come inside. "I'm waiting on the babysitters."

We walked into my living room, but before I could speak to him again, there was another knock at the door.

"Must be them." I smiled. "Excuse me a moment."

The baby and I went back to the door to let in my parents.

"Hi, thanks for coming." I smiled when I opened the door.

"Where's my sweet girl?" My mom cooed.

She had been the person I'd been most worried about when I had made the decision to adopt Oakley. She never thought I made the best decisions, and we had an awful relationship. I loved her, and I know in some ways she loved me, but we never saw eye to eye.

However, she accepted my adopted daughter almost instantly and hadn't done her typical fake an illness when life got too hard for her to handle. Since I was typically the source of her stress, I was glad this one thing I'd done had brought her joy.

I handed Oakley over, and she giggled when she realized who was holding her. She loved my parents.

"Aw, you love your Nanny, don't you?" Mom said.

"Hi, dad." I hugged him.

We all walked into the living room where Clint was. They hadn't met him before, so this should be interesting. I had hoped to keep him separate from them until I knew if we would be something more serious, if ever.

"Mom, Dad, this is Clint Hartley. Clint, my parents Babs and Charlie Webber."

"Nice to meet y'all." Clint extended his hand to both my parents.

"Nice to meet you as well." My dad said.

My mom smiled and then went back to playing with her granddaughter.

"Okay, so she had a bottle about forty minutes ago and should be good for a while." I said. "She's freshly changed too. Do y'all need me to show you where everything is?"

"Yes, please. As I'm sure I would never find anything. You don't do things the way I would." My mom said.

I just rolled my eyes and then showed her where everything was.

"I'm not sure how late we will be. The show starts at seven, so I should be back, what? No later than nine or ten?" I looked at Clint for reassurance. He nodded his agreement. "Any questions?"

"I think we'll be good, Jo." My dad said. "Have fun, kids."

"Yes, we'll be fine. We have raised kids before." My mom said.

"Okay, thanks."

Clint and I walked out. He held the door for me.

"Thank you, sir."

"Sir?" He chuckled.

"Just being silly."

He jogged around to the other side and climbed in.

"Ready?"

"Yep. I'm excited to see Fabio."

"Me too, even though I've seen it before. He always puts on a good show."

"Do you know much about him?"

"No, only that he does odd jobs and of course the magician gig. Why?" He turned his head slightly.

"No real reason. Just feels a little too obsessed. Fanboy-ish. You know? But I've only met him a few times."

"Ah, well, aren't you used to that? I know all the ladies in the garden club with my mom are obsessed with you."

"Ha, yeah, you'd think I would be, but I actually don't like that part of the job."

"Really?"

"Yeah, I just want to help people be at peace with their grief and have closure. I didn't get that with my husband. He died with this big secret. I would love to tell him off."

"Wow, I didn't know." He shrugged. "I hate to say this, but I thought you liked the drama."

"Seriously? That's funny."

"I'm sorry. I didn't know. Not offended?"

"Nah, not at all. Though, sometimes the drama-filled readings can be the most fun, but really, my favorites are when I can give the families peace and closure. All the love and fond memories make it worth it. That's the best feeling when you hear how happy they are to have those connections."

He nodded, and we let silence fall between us for a moment.

"You know my offer still stands to try to do a reading for you," I said after several minutes.

"Uh? Oh, no. I don't think I could. I wouldn't know what to say. Not after all this time."

"I understand." I really didn't, but didn't push it.

Personally, I would give anything to be able to have one last conversation with Ted, but then I didn't know the details of his situation. Maybe there was still too much pain there. Mine was painful, too, but I mostly wanted answers.

We pulled up to Barkers. I'd never been here before, but I'd heard it was an interesting place. We'd eat dinner, and then starting at seven, there would be stand-up comedians and magicians until Fabio's show. He was the headliner.

We got seated quickly and not far from the stage. I looked around at the quirky, unique décor. It looked like it had been decorated in the styling of an old circus sideshow, the kind that had the world's strongest man or the bearded lady.

Vintage circus posters hung in heavy wood and gold-trimmed frames, along with funhouse mirrors and replica props they might use. Framing the stage were thick purple velvet curtains tied back with gold tassels. The staff were dressed in various circus costumes, and all played the part well.

"This is an interesting place," I said as I picked up my menu.

"Very interesting."

We read over the menus, made our selections, and then placed our order with the waitress. She left some freshly baked bread and cinnamon butter. I had a weakness for warm bread, and all the best places served it, or at least in my opinion.

We each ate a slice of bread and chatted casually while we waited for our meals. We were still in the fun getting-to-know-you stage, so there were still a lot of childhood stories or 'this one time in college' moments to share.

Once we had eaten dinner and ordered a cocktail, it was time for the first performer to take the stage. We laughed along with the rest of the audience as the comedian told his tale of growing up in Creekview. It was funny because it was so relatable.

Another comedian took the stage, followed by a magician. This one wasn't quite as good as Fabio. He'd applied for the job but hadn't made it past the review stage. Still, he was entertaining but couldn't have held the stage for a full forty minutes as needed for our shows.

Finally, it was time for the main event, Fabio. I couldn't wait to see his full act in person.

He took the stage in full costume and tons of props. He started his act with some juggling, much like he'd done in my living room, but on a grander scale by getting a few people close to the stage involved. He made things 'appear' on their tables and asked them to throw it to him.

After that, he did a card trick. He asked the audience to shout out numbers, and he wrote a few on one of the cards. He then shuffled and flipped and shuffled some more. He did some other fancy finger work until he produced the card with the writing on it.

"Next up... wait a minute, folks. Do we have a celebrity in the house?" His eyes were on me. "It's Creekview's very own Joanna the Medium with a Heart."

Oh crap, I thought as all eyes turned to me, and a murmur started in the crowd. I put on my best stage smile and stood waving around the room. There were cheers, and a little crying started. That always happened. Grief was a weird thing bringing out a range of emotions.

"Should I bring her up on stage?" Fabio asked the eager audience.

The crowd went crazy. I tried to blow it off, but I gave in to the fans. I could feel my stage persona coming to the surface as I walked to join him.

"Thank you, all. I don't want to take away from the wonderful performers we have had here tonight." I said into the microphone that an employee handed me as I walked onto the stage. "Haven't they all been great? Let's give them all a round of applause."

The audience did just that, clapping and cheering, but then people started shouting for me to reach their loved ones.

"I want to speak to my mother. Her name's Tonia." One voice said.

"My father, Michael, would have been 100 today. Can you connect with him?"

"My great-aunt..."

"My sister..."

I heard so many voices. It was starting to become overwhelming. And if the living voices weren't bad enough, then the dead ones began in reply to some of the requests. I couldn't do this. My senses were overloaded, and the room started to spin.

"I'm sorry, everyone. That's not why I'm here." I looked over at Fabio and then down to Clint. "Let me give the stage back to Fabio."

Fabio mouthed he was sorry and started addressing the crowd, but I couldn't hear him over all the voices.

I swiftly walked off the stage, handing the mic back to the stagehand, and tried to make my way back to our table. However, people were starting to get up and mob me. Crowding around to the point I couldn't see Clint any longer.

"Clint?" I called out, then tried to push my way through the people. "I'm sorry, please, let me get back to my table."

I tried asking for people to let me by. I couldn't see anything above the crush of people. This had never happened before.

"Step back." I heard Clint's voice boom over the crowd, but people didn't move much.

We both kept working through the crowd to get to the other person. Relief filled my body when I finally saw his face. He grabbed me around the waist and guided me toward the door.

The club security guard also got to us and was able to hold back the mob to escort us to the door.

I was so thankful when we finally made it out and were safely back in his truck. With the crowd outside of it, I could breathe.

"Wow, that was crazy." He said, handing me my purse. "You okay?"

"Yes, yes. Thanks. I've never had that happen before."

"I'm glad I was with you."

"Me too. Thank you for saving me."

"My pleasure."

"I guess that's the end of this date."

"I guess so."

We drove back to my house relatively quiet, just the radio breaking the silence. We said goodbye at the door, and then I went in to relieve my parents of babysitting duty.

I hated how this date ended, but up to that point, it had been nice. Where do we go from here? Another date or call it quits? I didn't know how serious I wanted to get. Before adopting the baby, I rarely dated. Now with her, I had to reevaluate what I wanted.

Nothing had to be decided tonight, so I tried to put it out of my mind.

Chapter Thirteen

It was another week before I was finally visited by Macy, the most recent victim, and the waitress from Leo's.

"Hi, Joanna, I'm Macy." She appeared between clients.

"Oh, hi. How are you?" I cringed and did a mental facepalm. "I'm sorry, that's a dumb question."

"It's okay. This is all new to me too. I guess I'm alright considering."

"I guess you're here with information about your killer," I said.

"I'll try. I don't remember much because he drugged me. When he grabbed me, I got a slight look of an older man, thinning hair, but then he injected me with something, and everything got blurry and weird. Then I must have passed out. I woke up cold, wet, and in pain with my hands and feet tied. Oh, and I was blindfolded."

I exhaled sharply. This guy seemed to know how to keep his identity well hidden. What was he drugging them with? I'd have to ask Clint and Terry if they knew. I'm sure there had been autopsies. They probably couldn't tell me unless the media had released the information. I'd have to look because I don't remember seeing that in the stories I read.

She stood in front of me, nervously looking around. My heart went out to her. She was a few years younger than me but seemed far younger in the way she carried herself.

"So, no clues?" I finally said.

"I heard his voice. He kept ranting weird things."

"Ranting?"

She was the second one to say this.

"Yes, he seemed angry at someone. Saying 'She can't control me anymore' and then 'Why doesn't she notice me,' but I don't know who he was talking about. I tried to speak, but when I did, he hit me over and over until I passed out again. That was the last thing I remember."

A chill ran through my body. This guy was nuts. I thought again of my Grams's warning that someone was out to get me. Could it be this guy? I had a lot of physical features in common with the victims.

I wish she'd come back from wherever she is. I need more information, and she didn't have much to share on her visit.

Except for the similar physical features, there was nothing to suggest it was connected to me. There was no evidence or proof of anything at this point. It seemed I was letting paranoia take over.

Of course, Micah and I got locked in the abandoned building with a body who happened to be one of the victims. Then someone painted that word on my door. However, those could have been anything, right? It didn't necessarily mean this was the serial killer. Did it?

"I'm sorry. That sounds scary."

"I'm sorry and wish I had more to tell you, but I don't." She looked down and then up at me again. "I wanted to ask a favor, though. Could you talk to my boyfriend?"

"Oh, yes, of course." I pulled out a pen. "What's his name, and how do I find him?"

She gave me his name, his address, and told me he was one of Hank's guys. Of course, he was.

"Okay, so when should we go? I assume you want to be with me when I talk to him?"

"Oh, yes, please. I know you'll want to get a sitter, so I'll leave it up to you."

I checked my schedule. I could ask Janie if she was able to stay later tomorrow and then ask Micah or Tessa or both to go with me to Leo's. I liked to have someone with me for things like this.

"How about tomorrow after I finish work? Typically, between four and five."

"That's perfect. He'll be at Leo's. I can meet you there," she said.

"Great."

"Thank you for your help."

"You're welcome." I smiled.

She gave a quick wave and disappeared through a wall.

I stared at the spot in the wall for a minute, thinking about what she'd said. He'd been ranting some crazy things. Who was the 'she' he was referring to?

Thinking of Macy, the poor girl seemed lost and scared. I met a lot of dead people, and they all had varying reactions. I understood her reaction. She'd only been dead a short time, so it was still a new experience.

And while many had unfinished business, most had accepted their fate. Her situation was unfair. A life was stolen by a greedy bastard.

Micah and Tessa accompanied me to Leo's the next evening. Josh, Micah's boyfriend, wasn't able to join us as he usually would. He loved that part of our job, the part where he got to tag along and hear the drama and drink adult beverages. I admit that it was fun.

"Do you see Darius or Macy, boss?" Micah asked.

"Not yet," I said, glancing around the room. "Oh, yes, over there."

I pointed across to the far end of the bar. After Macy had left yesterday, I'd looked up pictures of her and Darius, so I knew who I'd be looking for.

He was downing a shot and had a few others lined up in front of him. Yikes, maybe this was a bad time.

I looked around for Macy to see if she was here. I didn't see her yet.

"No Macy yet. Let's go ahead and get a table while we wait." I said. "I'm starving."

My assistants agreed, and we found a booth. A waitress came over to take our order.

"Hi, I'm Lila. Oh, hey, Joanna, the medium!" She said excitedly, then a shadow crossed her face. "Are you here about Macy?"

"Yeah. She asked me to come speak to her boyfriend."

"Darius? I'd steer clear of him right now." She looked over her shoulder. "He's angry plus drinking, which is an ugly combo."

"Yeah, I see that."

"So, are y'all going to stay? I can take your drink order, if so."

I looked at my friends. They both nodded.

"Yes, thank you."

"Great, what can I get y'all?"

We placed our order, including some nachos. They had great nachos.

After Lila walked away, I looked around again and finally spotted Macy. She was standing near Darius, wringing her hands. She reached out to touch him, but of course, her hand went through him.

That's when she turned to look for me. Our eyes locked, and she waved and began making her way over.

I let my assistants know that Macy had walked over. They were getting used to me talking to ghosts they couldn't see.

"Hey, Joanna. I'm so glad you're here."

"Of course, happy to help in any way I can."

"I didn't know he'd be drinking so heavily, though." She looked back at him. "He isn't taking my death well."

We watched him down another shot and slam the glass down. He then looked around the bar, making eye contact with me. I looked away quickly, but it was too late. He was heading my way.

I watched from the corner of my eye as he stumbled over, pushing through a few people on his trek. They seemed to know him as none of them batted an eye. They simply helped him when he lost his footing a few times.

"Hey, hey... you're that Medium." He slurred out when he finally reached our table.

"Yes, I am. And you're Darius."

His eyes widened, and he pointed a finger at me. "Hey, how'd you know that?"

"I've been talking to Macy."

"Seriously?" He stammered. "What'd she say?"

I looked over at Macy. She was fidgeting. Even though I didn't know her before she'd died, I'd guess she had been a fidgeter, and this wasn't a new behavior.

"She says she misses you, and she's worried about you."

"Me? Why? I'm ff-fine..." But he didn't seem fine. He could barely say the word fine.

I looked at Macy again, listening to her words. I also caught the eye of Micah just to judge his reaction. He sometimes played bodyguard for me when we were on the road. Not that I'd ever been in real danger until recently. He was relaxed but watching closely, so I assumed he thought Darius was safe, or at least safe enough to keep talking to.

"She knows her death has been hard on you, and she wants you to know she's okay."

"Oh, she's okay, is she? She's dead. How's that okay?" He raised his voice. Several of Hank's other guys turned toward us but thankfully didn't come over. "I should have protected her. I shouldn't have let her leave alone that night, but Hank needed me. I asked her to wait until I was done working, but she left without me."

Tears formed in the corner of his eyes, then he slammed his hand down on the table. We all jumped and sat back from the table.

"She doesn't blame you. She said it was her choice to go."

"But..." He stopped and hung his head. "I'm going to get this effin guy."

I looked from him to Macy and then to my friends' faces.

"That's what I want to do as well. I'm working with the detectives to try to figure out who this guy is." I said.

"You are?"

"Yeah, so don't beat yourself up too much."

"I can't help it. She was the one."

Macy gasped when he said that.

"He was the one for me too," I told him her words.

He nodded. "I just feel lost without her, or you. Can I just talk to her? Is that a thing?"

"Yes, a lot of people just talk to their loved one, and I usually just speak exactly what they say, as if I'm them."

"Okay. Macy, I love you and miss you. It's only been a few days, but I know my life won't be the same without you." Tears rolled from his face, and he swiped them away violently.

"I love you too, Darius. You were my best friend and the love of my life."

He hung his head again and nodded. "Thank you, Joanna. This helps a little."

"I'm glad." I reached over and touched his hand. "She says she'll be close by, so you haven't completely lost her. She'll always be with you."

He looked up and gave a weak smile, then turned and stumbled back to the bar. One of his friends put his arms around his shoulder to comfort him while Darius laid his head on the bar.

I looked over at Macy. She followed him with her eyes. She clearly loved him. Would I ever find that type of love?

She turned back to me. "Thanks. I hope he feels better about this. It sucks."

She then walked away.

Nobody at my table spoke for several minutes until the waitress came over with our nachos, and it broke the silence.

"Wow, boss, that was intense," Micah said after the waitress was out of earshot.

"Yeah. I've never done a drunken reading like that."

"It didn't help with the case, though," Tessa added.

"Not at all, but I didn't think it would. This one was about closure, like what we do for everyone we do readings for."

I glanced across the room again to see Darius with his head still resting on his arms. His shoulders shook slightly as if he might be crying. It was heartbreaking.

We finished up our food and had another round before calling it a night.

After I got home, I settled into my regular evening routine of all things baby, including laundry, washing bottles, and watching Oakley play on the floor. My phone chimed with a text from Clint. I smiled as I read his simple message.

Good evening
Good evening to u
How's it going?
Oh, fun stuff. Laundry. U?
Nothing as exciting as laundry
Nothing is ever as exciting as laundry

We went back and forth, chatting a bit about nothing. By the time it was time for Oakley's bed, I was smiling.

After she was in bed, I decided to do some research again on the victims of this serial killer. The media was calling him the Playhouse Killer. I don't know how they come up with these names, but I knew it was supposed to be catchy and help the media have a reference for stories.

I just thought of the victims' families and friends. A playhouse was typically something happy, but this was meant horrifically. He used empty buildings, and it was like his "playhouse." Torturing his victims until they died. Alone, scared.

The few victims I had spoken to seemed okay, except for Macy. She wasn't at peace. She was worried about Darius. That was understandable.

Thinking about this, a chill ran down my spine. I'd been held in an empty warehouse once by a madwoman. She'd tied me up and held a gun on me. She then went into labor, and things changed. But for a brief moment in time, I thought I was going to die in that place, and I remember how scared I was.

On second thought, maybe I'd just go to bed. No more Playhouse Killer tonight.

Chapter Fourteen

I was working in my office with the baby asleep in the swing nearby. It was the weekend, so it should be quiet. No clients and most of the spirits that hung out weren't here.

While I was reading emails, my phone chimed. It was Clint. I smiled, reading this message, and then replying. We weren't planning to get together, but it was nice to have him think of me.

I hadn't dated in a while, maybe a year. Between my line of work and schedule, it always made dating a challenge. Guys either hated what I did for a living or couldn't handle my travel.

Now add in a baby, that might make things even more difficult. Despite knowing all those things about me, Clint still asked me out, so I wanted to see where it led.

I still wasn't sure what I wanted out of this relationship, but it was nice to have someone to talk to or go to dinner with here and there.

My phone chimed again. I was reading it when I heard a noise in front of me that caused me to drop my phone.

"Oh, I'm sorry. I didn't mean to startle you." The unfamiliar woman said.

"It's okay. I should be used to it." She was clearly a ghost because she was standing in my chair, as if she was part of the chair. "Can I help you? I'm not seeing clients today if you were hoping to meet with your loved ones."

"No, I came to speak to you. I'm Monica Eden. Clint was my fiancé."

"Oh, wow. Monica." I stumbled out. "Hi. Clint told me a little about you."

"He did?"

"Yes. Do you want me to call him? Do you have a message for him?"

"Oh, huh, no. I more wanted to just talk to you. Woman to woman." She smiled weakly. "Do you have time?"

"Yes, of course." I started to say, have a seat, but she couldn't.

"I know you are dating him, and I think it's wonderful." She said, which caused my face to warm. When you dated, it wasn't common for the ex to come around to talk to you. Unless it was in a threatening way, or maybe that was just my experience. "I'm so happy to see him dating someone, especially you."

"But you don't know me."

"I know enough. I've heard from others how much good you've done. You seem patient and caring. Clint needs that." She walked from the chair to the window. "He is such an old soul. You know what I mean?"

I nodded, but I wasn't sure if we had the same definition.

"He is sensitive, protective of those that he loves, and loyal almost to a fault." She turned to me. "He would give you the shirt off his back if you needed it. But he does try to hide his emotions and be a tough guy. That's primarily because of his job. He thinks being tough is how to be a detective, or when I knew him as a police officer."

She sighed and smiled. I guess remembering him back then.

"Yeah, I get that impression of him too." Though I used to think he was arrogant, I realized it was a facade he put up to protect himself.

"He needs someone who can be patient with him. He hasn't been able to commit to anyone since me. I know how broken he was when I died."

That explained a lot about him. I knew from talking to him that the pain of losing her was still acute even today.

"I'd offered to do a reading for him so y'all could talk. He didn't really turn me down, but he didn't accept either."

"I'm not surprised. He doesn't believe in this, or anything he can't prove or touch. I used to read him our horoscopes, and he'd just laugh at me."

"Yeah, he seems like he tolerates my job, and even though I've proven a few times that I am talking to spirits, he doesn't seem to believe."

We both laughed at that.

"He is just an analytical, logical thinker. Gosh, I miss him."

"So, do you have a message you'd like me to pass on to him?" I know I'd already asked, but I wanted to make sure she hadn't changed her mind.

She thought for a moment. "No, there's nothing I could say that he'd want to hear."

"Okay. I understand."

"I just wanted to share with you about Clint. He seems to like you, and I want him to find someone who can love him again. He deserves to be happy." She looked up and smiled. "I think that person could be you."

"Oh, wow. That's... thank you." What do you say to that?

"I'll let you get back to your day. Good luck." She smiled at me and then looked over at Oakley before leaving.

I sat there thinking about what she said. Was I the right person for Clint? Maybe, but the bigger question, at least in my eyes, was he the right person for me?

My life wasn't easy at times. I traveled several times a year for weeks at a time. There were fans, and I saw clients in my house, so little separation from work and life. Though I did try to find a balance that worked for me.

Then there was Oakley. She was a relatively easy baby, but raising a child with someone was going to be a commitment that a man would have to make. So, dating me also meant being involved in some ways with her.

I'm glad I got to speak to Monica, though. It gave me a better look at who Clint was. He was a complex person.

Oakley started to stir from her nap, so I shut down my computer. I'd come back to my email later. There were more important things to deal with now, like getting a clean diaper and warming a bottle.

Chapter Fifteen

It had been about a week since the incident at Barkers, and I was still shaking my head and wondering what had happened. I'd never had fans swarm me before. What had it been? Was it Barkers' freak show setting or the performers that put the people at ease? Whatever it was, I didn't like it, and even though I had enjoyed the food and entertainment, I doubted I would be going back there again.

I felt terrible for Fabio. I wonder what happened with his act after we left. The last thing I remember hearing before we fled was his voice over the speakers trying to get the audience's attention again and the words, "I'm sorry, Joanna."

I hoped that I hadn't ruined his night, or was it that he had ruined mine? Next time I saw him, I'd have to ask how it went.

I was lost in thought when my front door camera beeped, and then came a knock at the door. I wasn't expecting anyone, so I looked at my camera. It was some guy that I didn't know.

"Oh, wait. I think this is Brittney's boyfriend." I thought out loud.

Brittney was one of the victims. I was good at remembering facts, names, and faces. I'd looked through the ladies' social media enough to remember them and their various loved ones.

He knocked again. I couldn't decide what to do. Fake like I wasn't home? Crap, I knew I wasn't going to do that. One of my flaws, I was too curious and too nice. At least Janie had Oakley over at her house. That was a happy coincidence in case this went sideways.

I walked to the door and opened it halfway. "Hello? May I help you?"

"Yes, you're that medium, right? I have the right house?" He looked over his shoulder and then back to me.

"Yes, that's me. Can I help you with something?"

He stepped closer to me but then took a step back again. "Sorry, I just wanted to see if... I have questions. I tried making an appointment, but you're booked for months. I need answers now."

I looked at him for a moment, trying to decide what to do. I usually didn't take walk-in appointments, but maybe he could help with the investigation, and if I got to talk to another victim, perhaps it could help with the case.

"Okay, well, I have time at the moment, but there's no guarantee that your loved one or whatever spirit you're hoping to connect with will show up."

"Hmm, okay, I don't know how it works, but I want to try."

"Come in, and let's see what happens." I stepped back, so he could step inside. "Can I get you a drink? Water or a soda or something?"

"Water would be great. Thanks."

I nodded and gestured for him to have a seat in my office. When I returned with a glass of water, he was sitting in the side chair facing the window, so I took the one across from him.

"You're Matt, right? Brittney is who you want to speak to, yes?" I probably should have done a proper introduction before inviting him in, but again, I'm flawed in my trusting nature.

His eyes widened with surprise. "How'd you know? The news?"

"Yeah, the news." Biting my tongue that I was investigating the case and should be more careful with what I say.

He nodded. "So, anything yet?"

I looked around. There weren't any spirits here at the moment. They were all hanging out in the living room, and there were only a few today.

"Not at the moment, but I have a trick. Sometimes if I think about the person, like meditate, they will appear." Even though I wasn't sure if it actually worked, he didn't need to know that. "Perhaps we could both really focus on her."

We sat there silently, focusing. After a few seconds, he started tapping his fingers, so I lost some of my focus for a moment. Was he taking this seriously? Should I be worried that this was all a ploy to get in the house?

He fits Emma's super vague description of the Playhouse Killer. About 5'9" to 5'10". Slightly chubby, but not exactly fat. He had thinning dark hair. Could he be the killer? If so, it wouldn't be the first time I'd invited a killer into my home.

"Hmm, hello?" said a soft voice to my right.

I turned to see Brittney. Maybe this trick did work.

"Oh, hi, Brittney, right?"

"That's me." She smiled and did a half twirl.

"Brittney's here?" Matt perked up and stopped drumming his fingers.

"She is." I nodded to my right, his left side.

He looked. People always looked. I understood why. They all had hope that they would be able to see their loved ones themselves.

"What's she saying?" He asked.

"She says she misses you and is sorry."

"Sorry for what?"

"Sorry for... I don't know." I translated for her.

"I should be the one who's sorry. I wasn't there to protect you." His voice caught in his throat as he spoke. "Did you see him?"

"No, not well."

"Did you see him or not?" He asked sharply.

"It was dark and shadowy. He was kind of medium build, muscles, but not super tall." She thought for a moment. "He was a bit older, I think."

That fit Matt's description too. Goosebumps rose on my arms. Had I possibly invited another killer into my house? First Cate and now... well, there was no proof yet.

"Did he say anything to you?"

"I never heard him. He was quiet. Just could hear muttering but not enough to recognize the voice. Heck, at first I thought it was you doing a kinky sex thing, but then the pain started, and I knew it couldn't be you."

That made me almost sad and wanting to hug her. I didn't like this reading at all.

"How could you think I would do something like that?" He snapped.

"We'd talked about spicing things up a bit, and you liked blindfolding me, so I thought maybe."

This was a conversation best had privately and was making me a bit uncomfortable with their intimate talk. I understood, though, that I had to dictate her words so it couldn't be kept just between them.

"So, you're saying there is no way to ID this guy." He said again. It felt like he was fishing for something.

"I doubt it. It could literally be anyone with as much as I saw."

"Well, that's all I wanted to know. Obviously, she can't identify him, which is no help at all." He sighed. Was that a sigh of relief or frustration?

"Nothing else you want to say to her?" I asked, looking over at Brittney. She looked crestfallen. Even though ghosts don't have tears, she was crying. I wish I could comfort her in some way.

"Yeah, that's it. I'm just trying to help figure out who did this. She didn't see anything, so it's not helpful." His gruff tone caused me to wince.

He buried his face in his hands and made a low, frustrated scream sound, causing me to jump, and Brittney started sobbing louder.

"Sorry, I'm just frustrated." He finally said. "Thank you for your time. I'll leave you alone. I appreciate you taking a few minutes to talk to me."

I nodded and walked him out. Brittney followed behind him. I stood on the front step, watching Matt drive away when I noticed a familiar face walking across the street.

It was Fabio walking a couple of dogs. They looked like Mrs. Washington's pups.

He saw me and waved, then turned toward my house.

"Hey, Joanna." He called out as he stepped into my yard.

"Oh, hey, Fabio. What're you doing here?"

"I'm a dog walker." He grinned, looking down at the dogs. "These little guys are my new clients."

"Mrs. Washington's?"

"Yeah, aren't they the cutest?" He leaned over and scratched each behind the ears.

"Fun." I said. "So about the other night, I'm so sorry if I ruined your show. What happened after I left?"

"No, no problem. I should have known better. The crowd there can sometimes get out of hand, so I should be the one apologizing. I didn't think that through." He offered a smile. "It's just I saw you and was surprised you were at my show and let my excitement cloud my judgment."

"I've never had a crowd surround me like that. It was a bit scary."

"I'm sorry. I didn't mean to cause that." He said.

"I don't think you did. It was just a weird situation."

"Cool, cool. I'm glad you're okay, though."

"I'm glad you are too."

He smiled. "Okay, well, I gotta get their walk done. Take care."

He turned and walked back toward Mrs. Washington's house, and I got back to work. I had one more client to meet with, and then Janie would be bringing Oakley back.

It would just be me and my girl for the evening. I was looking forward to a nice, quiet night. Let's just hope it happened.

Chapter Sixteen

Today Oakley and I were meeting Laney and Aspen for lunch. We tried to get together a few times a month, but with newborns and jobs, it didn't always work out.

I arrived at Poppy's Bistro, our favorite place. Like usual, it was packed, but I managed to find a spot and then got Oakley's car seat unclipped. I got to the door just as Laney pulled in. I waved, then stepped inside to give our name, so we'd be on the list.

"Hey, Jo," Laney said, joining me inside a moment later.

"Hi." We hugged. "It's so good to see you."

"You too. Oh, look how big Oakley has gotten."

"And Aspen's outfit is adorable." She was wearing a light gray and white polka-dotted romper and soft tiny sandals.

Oakley had Cate's darker complexion and hair. Aspen was lighter, taking after Laney. Both girls had stunning blue eyes, which was clearly a trait they got from their father's side of the family. Other than that, they looked mostly like their mothers. You wouldn't guess they were sisters unless you knew.

"Thanks."

The hostess called for us, so we followed her to the table. They had turned the wooden highchairs upside down for us to put the girls' car seats into. It was perfect. Better than trying to balance on the tiny bistro chairs.

We got settled, and the waiter came to take our drink order.

"So, what's new with you?" Laney asked after skimming over her menu.

"Not much. Work and her."

"Gawd, I don't believe that at all." She smirked at me. "Rumor has it you've been out with a certain Detective."

"How the heck did you hear about that?"

"Greg saw y'all at Quench a week or so ago. He told me when he came to visit Aspen."

Greg was Laney's brother-in-law and also her ex-boyfriend. After her husband, Jeremy, died, she dated Greg for a short time. He was still in her life as uncle to Aspen. He'd softened a bit once she was born. Until that point, he had held a lot of anger toward his brother.

He was also technically Oakley's uncle as well but had only sent me a few emails asking about her or if he could get pictures for his parents. I think he only visited Aspen so he could see Laney.

"I didn't see him." I thought I had gotten more observant, but clearly, I hadn't. "So yes, I did go out with Clint. Actually, a few times now."

"Oh, really. Do tell." She leaned forward.

"Nothing much. The first time we had Oaky with us and the second time was dinner and then pool at Quench. It was also the night I came home to find the word bitch painted on my front door."

"What?" She gasped. I nodded. "Do you know who did it?"

"Not a clue."

"Wow, months ago, it was Cate and her goons terrorizing you, now someone else?"

During my investigation into Jeremy's murder, Cate had hired people to follow me and even break into my house.

"Looks that way."

"Any ideas who?"

"No, but I'm worried about it being related to the serial killer case."

"Seriously? Why?"

"I don't know, but all these things keep happening to me."

"It could just be a coincidence, right?"

"Of course, it could. It probably is." I honestly didn't believe it was a coincidence, but it helped me sleep at night.

The waiter brought our drinks and took our order. We changed topics to compare baby things, saving me from telling her about our third date. I still couldn't believe I had a baby, and my everyday conversations were around diaper changes, milestones, and onesies.

Both girls woke toward the end of our lunch, so we got them up and fed, changed, and then let them interact. It was sweet to see the little sisters smiling and cooing at each other.

Too soon, our lunch date was over, and it was time to go home.

"I'm glad we could do this again," Laney said when we were outside.

"Me too. Next time play date at my house."

"Definitely."

We hugged and said our goodbyes.

After I left Laney, I had to stop by the grocery store. Halfway through my shopping, I heard a familiar voice call out to me.

"Hey, Joanna." It was Fabio.

"Oh, hi, Fabio."

"How's it going? Oh, here's your baby. She's so cute." He gushed.

"Um, thanks." I beamed at my daughter, who was staring wide-eyed at the stranger. "So, what're you doing here?"

Awkward question alert. Duh Jo, it's a grocery store, I thought.

"Grocery shopping." He said with a laugh.

"Yeah, sorry, that was obvious. I guess just meant, how are you?"

"Good, I'm good." He bounced slightly as he spoke. "I had a gig last night, no swarming crowds this time. I practiced some new material, the stuff I'm hoping to use on the road for your show. It went over well."

"Nice." I looked around for a reason to excuse myself.

"Yeah, it was one of my best shows."

"Oh, that's great. Not like the night I ruined it." We both laughed a little. It had been a scary moment, but I could joke about it a bit.

"You didn't ruin anything. You're wonderful."

That sobered my mood. I shifted under his gaze.

"Oh, and everyone was excited to hear I would be opening for you. There were big cheers." He said proudly.

"Wait, what? Didn't Micah tell you? We have to do an official announcement. Nothing is supposed to be out about our tour until then. It was in the contract."

"Oh, I missed that. I'm sorry."

"Please don't share anymore until we give you the word." Had we made a mistake with this guy? He didn't seem professional at all.

"I'm sorry. I'll take down everything from my social media too."

"Please do." I snapped a little too harshly.

Thankfully, Oakley picked that moment to start whining.

"I better get my shopping done before she really starts crying," I said quickly.

I hurried away and blazed through the store, trying not to forget the most essential of things, diapers, in my rush. Oakley was a laid-back baby, but when she got upset, it was hard to get her to stop.

Thankfully, we made it through without a complete meltdown. She waited until we got into the car. I decided to drive around until she calmed down or at least until I needed to get the groceries home. I figured a few extra minutes wouldn't hurt.

I pointed the car on the long path home. I talked quietly and calmly to her from the front seat. It only took five blocks for her tantrum to simmer down, and she fell right to sleep.

Once it was quiet, I thought about my encounter with Fabio. Had Micah not gone through the contract with him well enough? I knew we didn't hire people regularly, but when we had discussed it, that part was his idea. No, I knew he had gone through it, and it was Fabio who hadn't held up his end of the bargain. Whether intentional or not, I didn't like that.

As I turned toward home, a movement behind me caught my eye. A car was a little close to me. Of course, my mind went straight to the worst-case. I was being followed.

I took a right at the next street, and so did the car, then I went right the next street. The car did the same.

"Crap." My mind went into overdrive.

I took a few more random turns, but the moment I was about to hit the panic button and call the police, it turned into a driveway.

"Ugh, I'm a paranoid mess." I chastised myself and then made my way home.

We made it without further worry, and the rest of our evening was uneventful unless you count Oakley rolling from front to back and then back to her stomach again. She was getting this rolling thing down.

Chapter Seventeen

Today I was going to visit Caitlyn in jail. This would be only the second time since she'd been locked up that I've been able to visit her. It would be a special one as I was finally able to bring Oakley with me. I knew it was heartbreaking for her to not raise her daughter, but Cate had taken three lives and understood her guilt.

At least she was remorseful. I'd never known anyone else charged with murder, so I didn't know how others felt about their crimes, and whether this was a normal feeling or not.

I dressed the baby in a pink and gold-trimmed dress that Cate had bought months before when she still thought she would get to raise her own daughter. I added a soft headband with a bow. She didn't have much hair yet, just wisps of soft dark hair.

After she was ready, diaper bag packed, and a few comfort items that I had been approved to bring to Caitlyn, I loaded everything into the car.

"Alright, baby girl, let's go see your first mommy," I told her as I buckled her in.

As I drove across town, I was running through the list of victims for this serial killer case. I couldn't believe we still didn't have any leads. Nothing. Nobody. It was frustrating.

No new victims had visited me, and none of the others had returned. They didn't have reliable information before, so I doubted they had anything new.

I was lost in thought, but a sudden movement in my rearview mirror caught my eye. A car had gotten too close.

"Back off, buddy," I mumbled and then tried to speed up slightly. When I did, so did the car. "What the heck?"

I sped up a little more, it sped up. I changed lanes, it changed lanes. Panic spread through my body.

Unlike with the other cars that weren't really following me, this one was mimicking my movements. This must be the real deal.

I drew from my previous experience with being followed by making some random turns, even going back in the direction of home, just to see what would happen. The strange car stayed right with me.

I tried in vain to see who was driving, but there was a glare across their windshield. I just tried to focus on staying on the road, not freaking out, and continued toward the jail, even if on a strange path.

After a few miles, I got to the point that my panic overtook me, especially as it sped up, getting too close for comfort. I decided I needed to do something different.

"Call Clint," I said to my phone. It connected via the car's speakers.

"Hello."

"Clint, someone is following me."

"Are you sure? What makes you think that?"

"It has been behind me for nearly ten minutes. I have been trying to shake it, driving a crazy path. It's like when Cate's guys were following me, except this one is a little aggressive."

"Aggressive? What do you mean?"

"They keep speeding up on my tail and then backing off. Or when I change lanes, they do too."

"Okay, okay. Where are you?" There was some fumbling on his end.

"I was heading to see Cate, but I'm... oh gosh, where am I?" I'd been so focused on keeping my eyes on the car, I'd lost track of which street I was on. "I'm on Becker near the high school."

"Okay, just head toward the jail, since you're only a few miles away. I'll meet you there."

"Can you stay on the phone with me, please? I have the baby with me, and I'm trying to stay calm."

"Yeah, not a problem." I could hear the jingle of keys and then him moving through the station. "Is the car still with you?"

"Hmm." I looked back. "Yes, right on my tail. I swear they must be inches from me, but I don't understand why."

"Could be road rage?"

"Maybe, but I don't think I did anything to them. They came out of nowhere."

I really racked my brain to think if I might have cut someone off by accident, or had I not stopped at a stop sign? Was I going too slow at any point? I couldn't think of anything, but that doesn't mean I didn't. My mind had been in a million different places.

He kept talking calmly to me as I drove, and finally, the county courthouse came into view. I was here. There would be lots of people and various law enforcement.

"Okay, I'm here. I'm parking in the lot on Elm and Second street."

"Great. I'm two blocks away." He said a low curse. "Sorry, got caught at a light. Is the car still with you?"

As I pulled into the lot, it slowed and then revved the engine, squealing the tires as it took off.

"Wow, was that the car?" He asked.

"Yep, they're gone." My body went liquid with relief. I'd been followed before but having Oakley with me was a different kind of fear and vulnerability. "I'm going to park as close to the door as I can. Wait, is that you?"

He pulled his truck up next to mine, so I put my window down. Tears of relief formed in my eyes at the sight of him.

"I've never been so happy to see you. I was terrified."

"I'm sorry." He looked around. "Park over there. I'll meet you."

I pulled into the spot Clint pointed out and watched as he parked a few spaces away from me. He jogged over, opening my door when he reached it. I stepped out and into his arms. My body started shaking, and the tears that had formed in my eyes fell onto his shirt.

"I was so scared."

"I've got you now. You're okay." He said so softly and sweetly.

"I wasn't even worried about me. It's Oakley." I looked over my shoulder at my car. She was fine, but what if that person had decided just following wasn't enough. I couldn't even voice this worry to Clint. Call me superstitious, but saying it out loud made it feel like it would come true.

My breathing evened out, and the tears dried. I loosened my hold on Clint and stepped back slightly.

"Better?" He asked.

"Yes, thank you." I smiled at him. He kissed my head.

"Do you want me to stay with you for the visit? I don't have to go in when you see Cate, but I'll just stay nearby."

"Can you? What about work?"

"This is part of my job. Protect and serve." He chuckled. "Plus, nobody in town would let me live it down if anything happened to our town celebrity."

"Ha ha, but okay."

I know I had some celebrity status, but I was not so arrogant to think I was owed special treatment for it. My dad, on the other hand, really enjoyed the free coffee he got at his favorite diner.

I got the stroller out of the trunk, unclipped Oakley's car seat, then clipped it in the stroller. Grabbing the bag, my purse, and the items for Cate, I was all set.

"All of this for a baby?" He raised his eyebrows.

"Yeah, babies have a lot of stuff, but this bag is for Cate." I held up the bag with her things in it. "A few things they said I could bring her. A few books, some special toiletries. Things like that."

He nodded.

"So, did you happen to get a good look at the car?" He asked.

"It was a dark green sedan of some sort, but there was a glare in just the right spot that I couldn't see the driver or the make. I'm not even sure if it was just one person or more than one. Male or female? I'm sorry. I tried to get those details."

"It's okay. It happens. Plus, I know you were nervous about the baby."

We got checked in, going through the security checks, and then I was escorted to the room to meet with Cate. Clint stayed behind as discussed.

I unbuckled Oakley from her car seat and held her as I waited for Cate. I couldn't even think about how important this moment was for her. While I was still worried about who was following me, I wanted to be in the moment for both mother and daughter.

"Jo! Hello!" Cate's bubbly voice filled the room as the door came open to my left. "Oh, she's gotten so big."

I stood and handed the baby over to her biological mother. We both had tears in our eyes.

We didn't speak while Cate cuddled Oakley, talking softly and lovingly to her. She loved her daughter. Oakley stared at her with curious eyes but quickly warmed up to her and grabbed at her face, cooing.

"She's so perfect, Jo. Thank you for taking her and raising her."

"It's been my pleasure. She's such a sweet baby, and everyone who meets her loves her."

"Oh, that makes me so happy." Cate looked down adoringly at our daughter. "So how are you doing?"

"I'm okay. Work has been busy, but good." I smiled, trying to ignore the scary moment just before walking in here. "How are you doing? You okay?"

"Um, yeah, I'm okay. I mean, as good as I can be." She touched her hair. "Going back to my natural color. No more blonde." Her hair was a chestnut color and cut into a bob. Before her arrest, she'd worn it long and bleach blonde.

"I like this style on you, though."

She laughed. "It goes well with the beige jumpsuit."

"A little bit." We shared a laugh.

"Anything else exciting? Are you just doing medium work, or did you switch over to crime-fighting?" She asked. "If not, you should. You really were close to figuring me out."

"Um, I'm still doing medium work, but actually, I'm also helping on another case." I paused, fidgeting with my shirt. I wasn't sure if I should tell her, but maybe she might have some insight. "Have you heard of that serial killer, the Playhouse Killer?"

"OMG, are you working on that?" She looked down at the baby. "You need to be careful. That guy is terrifying."

"Yeah, things have gotten scary. I was followed here." I didn't mention yesterday because that was just me being paranoid.

"What?" She blurted out, startling the baby. "Oh, shh, shh. I'm sorry."

Oakley cried harder and looked around as if for me, so Cate handed her over. I patted her back and cooed to her until she quieted.

"I'm sorry. So, what happened?" She asked quieter this time.

"Yeah, somebody followed me, but I got here, and Clint is outside, so I should be okay. It was frightening, though, especially having her with me."

"I bet." She looked down at the baby now in my arms. "I'll tell you now, I don't have anyone following you. There is no reason for me to do that. There really wasn't before."

"I assumed it wasn't you, but I have no idea who it could be. I haven't talked to anyone. Just the victims. They're all spirits, so it's not like they can tell anyone."

"True." She tickled the baby's foot. "You don't think it's the serial killer following you, do you?"

"I guess I thought maybe, but why?"

I might have had that thought too, but hearing someone else say it, especially someone who had planned and pulled off murders, made it more of a possibility in my mind.

"I had people follow you, so I'd know what you were doing and when and with whom."

Yikes. Maybe I should get a gun or a scary dog or both. Perhaps I should move and change my name.

A guard stepped in and gave us the five-minute warning.

"Oh gosh, this visit wasn't long enough. Please say you'll come back soon." Cate said with new tears forming in her eyes. "I miss her so much, but I know she's in the right place. She's clearly thriving with you."

I handed the baby back to her for the last few minutes, so she could soak up some last hugs and kisses, along with that sweet baby smell.

"Time's up." The guard announced.

We hugged quickly, and that was it. She was back behind the four walls of the jail. She had given me something to think about, though, and I'd have to be much more aware of my surroundings.

Chapter Eighteen

Today was my day off, so I went over to Audrey's house to visit with her and let the boys see their cousin. We had always been close, and now that I had a baby, we had one more thing to bring us closer.

I pulled up a little before nine. I got the baby and her bag, then walked up to the front door.

Audrey opened it as soon as I reached her steps, followed by her boys. I loved that my family was so excited about my daughter.

"Oakley!" Harris and Dylan called out, trying to peer into the car seat.

"Boys, let's let Auntie Jo get in the house, and we can get Oakley out of her seat," Audrey said with a laugh.

We walked to her family room, and I unclipped Oakley. Audrey had laid out a blanket on the floor, so I put the baby down. She immediately started scooting around and trying to get to Harris.

"She likes me!" He squealed and got down to play with her. "Here, baby. Come to your cousin."

"Here, baby," Dylan said, copying his big brother.

"Don't crowd her." Audrey told the boys. "Let her move around."

I pulled out a few toys I'd brought for her and spread them around. She giggled and went for her favorite little monkey. When she reached it, she rolled onto her back with it going right to her mouth.

"She is getting so big, Jo." Audrey commented, then asked. "Coffee?"

"Yes, please."

We stepped a few feet away to her kitchen. She had a great setup with her open concept. The kitchen and family room were open to each other so the kids could be seen while we sat at her kitchen bar sipping coffee.

"So, Stan and I were wondering if you and Clint would want to go out together. Double date?"

"Oh, gosh, I don't know. We aren't very serious."

"Are you serious enough to go to dinner? I mean, it's just dinner."

"Ha, okay. I'll ask him."

I fired off a text and got a near-instant reply.

"He said sure, when?"

"I can ask my babysitter when she's available. I'm sure she can watch Oakley too." Audrey started typing a text.

I watched the boys playing with Oakley. "I never thought this would be me." I gestured toward them.

"I'm so glad you adopted her. It's been so great watching you grow into this role. It fits you well."

"Aw, thanks, sis."

Her phone chimed. "She can watch them all anytime. How about tonight?"

We both started texting and making plans. Soon it was set. We'd have a double date tonight. Yikes. Why had I said yes? That seemed like something you do when you are in a more serious relationship. Maybe I was and didn't realize it.

We spent a couple of hours with my sister and her family before I left to let Oakley nap. Then I'd get dressed for the date and grab more supplies for Oakley. I was a bit nervous but excited.

I watched for any cars following me, and I was careful with my driving just in case it had been road rage. If someone were targeting me, I couldn't control that, but I could control my driving.

We got home, and I put the baby down for a nap. Then I went to my closet.

"What to wear? What to wear?" I flipped through my clothes.

Around the house, I typically wore jeans and t-shirts or casual style blouses. When I saw clients, I had a lot of flowy blouses and dresses. Then for the stage, I had even more flashy outfits. I needed to find something in between.

I settled on a mustard yellow floral banded waist maxi dress with cap sleeves, pairing it with dark brown strappy sandals with just a slight heel. I did a soft curl to my hair and put on a touch of makeup, keeping it natural with soft skin tone colors.

Once I was dressed, I packed Oakley's formula and bottles, diapers, and extra baby wipes. Then made sure there were a couple of extra outfits, just in case.

When all that was ready and the baby was awake, we headed back over to Audrey's. The baby happily cooing as we drove over. I was too nervous but tried to focus on driving and not the double date or the fact I may or may not be in a serious relationship.

"Oh, sis, you look amazing," Audrey said when she opened the door.

"So do you." She was wearing a navy-blue striped jumpsuit with red pumps.

"Thanks. I love this outfit, but I hope I don't have to pee. It's a pain to get off." She laughed.

"I bet."

Before we were inside her house, Clint pulled up. He hopped out and jogged over.

"Hey, ladies." He kissed my cheek when he reached me.

"Hey to you. Good timing. We just got here." I said.

"Hi, Clint." Audrey said. "Come on in, y'all."

We followed her inside, and I unclipped the baby from her car seat, placing her on the blanket in the family room. I spread her toys around. My nephews came running from upstairs.

"Baby Oakley's back!" Harris yelled. He laid down next to her, and she giggled then grabbed his face. "She likes me so much."

"She does," I said, touching my nephew's head. He beamed up at me and then went back to his little cousin.

Stan came into the room and shook Clint's hand. The guys started talking about sports. I went over the instructions quickly with the babysitter. She seemed like a nice kid.

"Are y'all ready?" Stan asked.

"Yes." We all said.

We planned to dine at Griffin's Steakhouse. We opted to travel together in one vehicle, so we all got into Stan's car.

"You look nice," Clint whispered to me once we were settled in the backseat.

"So do you," I replied.

He was wearing a navy plaid sports coat with a pale blue shirt, a dark gray tie with slacks the same color as the tie. I'd never seen him so dressed up. He typically wore a polo shirt with khakis.

"Who knew you were such a fashion-forward dresser?" I said coyly.

"I'm trying a new thing." He laughed.

We pulled up a few minutes before our reservation. The hostess asked us to wait just a moment and then seated us. This place was classy. I had only been here one other time, and it was years ago.

"This place is nice. Thanks for suggesting it, Stan." I said.

"Not a problem. We love it." He replied. "Normally, we come for our anniversary but figured it would be a good double date place."

Clint looked over at me with a smile. I hope he didn't think I was more serious about this than I was. If only I could read minds, not just speak to the dead.

We had a lovely meal and great conversation. Overall, it was a fun, successful date. I was thankful for my sister and brother-in-law for suggesting this, and I was more thankful nothing crazy happened on this one.

Chapter Nineteen

I woke with a start at two in the morning. Rubbing my eyes, I sat up to try to figure out what had awakened me. I didn't hear the baby on the monitor.

My blood ran cold when I realized what I was hearing. Someone was inside my house. I could hear footsteps and someone opening cabinets.

My next thought was getting to Oakley. I jumped out of bed, then rummaged around for a weapon. Sadly, the only thing I came up with was my slipper. What I planned to do with it, I had no idea. Slap someone, I guess.

Still, I clutched that pink slipper like a lifeline as I slowly made my way across my bedroom, taking a deep breath as I slowly turned the doorknob to my room.

I had no plan, just knew I had to get across the house to Oakley's room. As I stepped into the hallway that leads to the kitchen, I could see the back door was ajar. Why hadn't my alarm gone off? This was the second time that it hadn't worked.

I also realized I should have grabbed my cell phone, not just this useless slipper. I peeked around the kitchen. Nobody. I tiptoed into the living room without seeing anyone. I made it to the hallway that leads to Oakley's room when I heard something in my office. I sprinted as quietly as possible into her room.

Heading straight to her window, I unlocked it and slid it open. Then I carefully picked her up, dropping the slipper. I climbed out the window, cradling her as gently as I could. Again, I had no plan, but we were out of the house and away from whoever was in there.

Oakley started to cry. I needed to get away from the house, but I couldn't think. I ran down the street and hid several houses down near the park.

"Shh, Oakley. It's okay." I rubbed her back.

Suddenly, there was a figure next to me. I screamed.

"Ms. Joanna, it's okay. It's me, Eddie."

It was one of Hank's guys. I sighed with relief.

"Oh, thank gawd, Eddie. Someone's in my house."

"I'm on it, but first, come with me." He walked me over to a dark SUV that I hadn't even noticed and opened the back door. In the driver's seat was Al. "Al, there is someone in her house. I'm going to check it out."

Eddie grabbed something from the front seat, I'm guessing a gun. Then I watched his dark figure creep down the street toward my house and then disappear around the back.

"I'm so glad y'all were here. I was so scared." I said to Al.

He simply nodded.

"I didn't know you would be one of the guys watching my house."

He grunted.

"I do really appreciate it."

He didn't even acknowledge that, so I decided to give up. We sat in silence. The only sound was Oakley's occasional whimper. Several minutes ticked by as we waited.

Finally, Eddie came back.

"It looks clear. I called the police, and they are on their way to take a report."

"Thank you so much." I started to get out of the car.

"No, wait for the police to get here. We'll stay with you until they arrive."

Thankfully, the baby had fallen back to sleep in my arms as we waited. Eddie made small talk in the front seat while Al just nodded along in response to Eddie's babble. I stared out the window. How was this my life?

Finally, the police showed up, including Clint and Terry.

Clint stepped out of the car and came straight to me, wrapping his arms around me.

"Thank you for coming. Why are you here? I didn't think this was your type of call, and it's late." I had just seen him a few hours ago. I didn't realize he would be working late, or I wouldn't have asked him to go out.

"Yeah, Terry and I were working a lead when the call came in."

"Ms. Webber?" the uniformed officer said. "We need you to look around, see if anything is missing."

Eddie and Al stayed outside so they could give statements to the police, but Eddie told me they would be close by.

I nodded to Eddie, then followed the officers inside. At first glance, nothing looked out of place, but the office was dark, and that is where the thief had been.

"I need to lay the baby down first, if that's okay?"

They nodded. Clint followed me back to the bedroom. He checked the window, relocking it from when I climbed out. Oakley squirmed a little as she resettled into her bed.

I watched her a moment and then turned to Clint.

"I was so scared. All I could think of was getting to her." I whispered.

"I can imagine."

We went back out to the living room to join Terry and the other officer.

"I did a perimeter check. Found this. I assume it's yours." Terry said, handing me my slipper. I nodded, taking it from him. "Your security camera is disconnected."

"Seriously? That's the second time." I blurted.

"I'm going to look at it," Clint said.

"Do you want to check in your office?" Terry suggested. "That's where you said the perp was, right?"

"Yes. At least when I ran through here."

They followed me down the hall to my office. Flipping on the light caused me to gasp as I took in the sight of all my things strewn around the room.

"What a mess." I said.

"I'm sorry, Jo," Terry said, putting his hand on my shoulder to comfort me.

I started sifting through the mess, making note that a few knickknacks were missing, but nothing valuable. It didn't make sense. Why would someone do this?

Last time this kind of thing happened, I was actively talking to suspects in the case. This time I'd only spoken to a few people. Two of the boyfriends and Hank plus the victims, but they couldn't talk to anyone. That's it. I know Hank wouldn't have done this to me.

"So, anything missing?" Clint asked, stepping into the office.

"A few trinkets, but nothing of value," I said, choking on the words. "Who would have done this to me again? I try to be a good person."

A few tears spilled. Clint put his arms around me, and Terry patted my arm. The uniformed officer cleared his throat and left the room. Terry squeezed my arm once and then followed suit.

"I'm so sorry this keeps happening to you." Clint whispered. "This doesn't mean you did anything wrong. This person did."

"I know that logically, but it's just scary, especially now with Oakley." I said, grabbing a few tissues from the box on my desk. "I know I keep saying that, but it's true. She can't do anything to protect herself. It's my job to do that for her, but I feel like all I'm doing is putting her in danger."

"I'm sure it feels like that, but it's not true. You are doing the best you can. And look, I'm here. There are a lot of people here to protect you and her."

I tried to smile, but I didn't quite feel it. What was I going to do?

"Maybe I should get a dog." I mumbled absently.

"That's actually a good idea."

"I'm seriously considering it. If I had a dog, it could've barked to either deter the burglar or to at least alert me to the stranger. It would have changed how things went tonight."

He nodded. Terry came back in to say they had finished gathering prints. He would wait outside for Clint as they had driven together.

"Do you want me to stay with you?"

"No, you don't have to. I'm sure I'll be fine." Honestly, I wouldn't be able to sleep, but I didn't tell Clint.

"Are you sure?"

"Yeah, I'm sure whatever they were after, they got and won't be back."

"Probably so. But if it ever happens again, will you please remember your phone?"

"Yeah, that was really dumb."

I walked him out, said goodbye to both him and Terry, and then locked the door behind them. I made a beeline for the baby's room. She was sleeping peacefully.

I checked her window. Locked. I then walked around the entire house checking windows and doors, even though I know both Terry and Clint had done it.

I grabbed my phone and pulled up the app for my security system. Clint had been able to reconnect it. I flipped through the various camera views. Nothing.

"It's going to be a long night."

I checked the clock to see it was nearly five a.m. Not night any longer, but early morning. No point in even trying to sleep. I went straight for the coffee pot. I'd need it to get through the day.

I'd have to research a new security system. Clearly, this one wasn't ideal. That would at least help take my mind off of the break-in and waste some time until a more reasonable point of the morning.

Chapter Twenty

I rubbed my thumb across the candle holder I stole from Joanna. I had gotten a few things, but this little teal votive was my favorite item.

I hadn't meant to scare her. Darn, I just wanted something of hers. I thought I could get in and out without anyone knowing, but then when I realized she woke up, I got sloppy. Making a mess had not been the plan.

Having a few of her things dampened my frustrations and need to hurt. I didn't want to get caught and didn't want to kill again. Being near her made me happy, and that urge to hurt, to cause pain, wasn't as intense.

Next, I picked up the ceramic bird I'd grabbed.

"This is cute." I turned it over in my hand and looked around each side. "Actually, you might be my favorite."

I had wanted to get something a bit more personal, but the little trinkets were all I had time for. When I heard her run across the living room, I knew I had to be quick, and I just started grabbing.

And dammit, I hadn't realized Hank the Hammer had guys watching her. I'd have to be more careful. I might be able to take out some small women, but Al was a different story. He was not someone I wanted to tangle with.

I played with the little bird, then drifted off to sleep holding it tightly as I dreamed of a certain brunette with the beautiful smile.

Chapter Twenty-One

~Joanna~

A few days later, I had some time off, so I asked Janie to watch Oakley, so I could go to the animal shelter. I had thought it over, and I needed to get a dog. We'd had a couple of dogs growing up, but this would be my first as an adult.

"So, what are you thinking? Big or small?" Audrey had joined me to help me decide.

"I don't really want one too big, but not small either. Maybe a medium-ish one? No more than maybe fifty to sixty pounds. What size is that?" I was filling out the application.

"I think that's considered large, but I'm not an expert." She chuckled. "Boy or girl?"

"Honestly, that doesn't matter as much as size and temperament."

"Maybe I can talk Stan into getting us a dog too." She said, almost giddy.

"Your boys would love a dog."

Once I was done with the application, I went up to the counter. She thanked me and said someone would come to take me back soon.

"I can't believe you had another break-in," Audrey said.

"I know. This one was scarier because I was home and of course, I have the baby now. I felt so helpless."

"Motherhood will do that, but I'm sure the mother bear instinct would have kicked in."

"Joanna?" A woman said from a side door. "Follow me."

She led the way to the back. The sound of barking grew louder, and the smell of wet dog got intense. Maybe this wasn't a good idea. I didn't like all the barking or the smell. But then, I reminded myself that there were several dozen dogs here, not just one. One probably wouldn't be as bad as all these dogs.

But I did note that the facility itself was clean.

"I'm Lina. I see you're looking for a medium to large-sized dog and about a year old."

"That's right. I have a young baby, so I don't want to have to deal with the puppy stage. Plus, I'm hoping one that is good with kids."

"Great. I have a few that might fit." She opened the door to a large room. It was lined on each side and down the middle with what could only be described as doggy jail cells. There was at least one dog in each dog kennel. Some had two.

We walked past a few, until stopping at a kennel with a small gray and white dog in it.

"This is Smitty. Part lab, part pit bull. And I know people think pits have a bad rep, but this guy is a doll. His owner ran a daycare, but sadly she died suddenly."

Smitty had a huge grin and a wiggly butt. "He's cute for sure. How old?"

"He's almost four."

"Okay." I looked at him for a moment. "I'll keep him in mind. You said you had a few others. Maybe a little younger?"

"Yes, right here." She took a step to the right. "This is Stevie. She's a German shepherd mix. Roughly two years old. Not sure about kids, only because she hasn't been around them, but she's very gentle."

I looked at the brown-eyed beauty. She wagged her tail but otherwise didn't move from her seated position.

"She's cute." Audrey said. "And looks sweet."

"She does."

We walked a few kennels down to a black and white dog, then to a brown and white one. Then several more as they started to blur together.

"Any that you'd like to meet in our private room?" Lina asked.

"Um." I looked around the vast room. I had no idea. There were so many to choose from. "Maybe Stevie and Chewy?" Chewy was a chocolate lab mix that was a little over a year old.

"Good choices. We'll get Stevie out first. Let me show you to the room." As we walked by Stevie's kennel, Lina unlocked it and hooked a leash on her. Stevie calmly followed her.

Lina led us all into a door outside of the kennel area and then down a hallway. It all seemed sterile and plain. White linoleum flooring, plain cream-colored walls with a random poster here and there. The smell of dog wasn't as strong the further we got away from the kennel area.

"Here we go." She opened the door to a room. There were a couple of chairs and a sink. "Wash your hands, and then she's all yours."

She leaned over and unhooked Stevie's leash. Audrey and I both washed our hands and then lowered ourselves to the floor.

"Here, Stevie," I said with my hand out.

She sniffed in my direction but then looked over her shoulder toward Lina. Lina encouraged her. Stevie replied with a wag of her tail and then sat down.

Audrey tried calling her but nothing. Stevie laid down and yawned.

"She doesn't seem interested in us at all."

"She's calm, though," Audrey said.

"That's true. Very calm." I noted.

"Stevie, come on, girl. You're never going to get a home this way." When Lina moved toward her, Stevie perked up.

"I think she likes you." I pointed out.

"Yeah, but I can't adopt anymore. I already have three." Lina scratched the mutt's head. "Okay, I'll take her back and get Chewy."

She left, and Audrey and I sat there. We chatted quietly while we waited. After only a few minutes, Lina returned.

"Okay, here's Chewy," Lina said, stepping in being pulled by the sixty-pound puppers.

"Hi, Chewy," I said. He came bounding over, all tongue and tail. "Wow, this is much different than Stevie. Good boy."

I scratched his head, and he climbed into my lap, rubbing all over me. After a few pets, he settled happily and calmly in my lap. He kept looking up at me with what could only be described as a puppy grin.

"I think he likes you, Jo," Audrey said, reaching over and rubbing his belly. He moved just enough to lick her hand. "He's sweet too."

"He is." I looked up at Lina. "Sorry, I don't remember, did you say if he was good with kids?"

"Not sure. He hasn't been around them. If you'd like to bring your baby here to meet him, you can, before making a final decision."

I nodded. "I wonder if we should bring Harris and Dylan too. They'd be a good test as well. If they were to run around, we'd see how Chewy would act around them."

"Yeah, that's a good idea." Audrey agreed.

"Great. You can come back today or tomorrow. Depends on how quickly you'd like to adopt." Lina said.

"Let me call my babysitter and see if she can bring Oakley up here. Do you think Stan could bring the boys?" I asked Audrey.

"Yeah, I'm sure he can."

An hour later, all the kids, Stan, and Janie had joined us in the little room. Chewy loved the attention. He was bouncing around between each person, chasing without jumping on the boys, smelling without licking Oakley, and greeted each person without jumping on them.

"He is the politest puppy I've ever met." Janie said. "You said he's only a year old?"

"That's right. We have a great dog trainer here. He works with all the new dogs." Lina said.

"So, what do y'all think?" I asked the group.

"You've gotta get this dog, Auntie Jo," Harris said, hugging Chewy around the neck. Chewy grinned and licked Harris' face.

"I agree. I think I'll adopt him." I looked over at Lina. "When can I take him home?"

"He can actually go today. We're so overcrowded. Plus, he's already fixed and up to date on shots."

"Really? I'd love to take him today." I rubbed behind his ears.

"Awesome. I'll go work up his adoption papers."

A few hours later, we were settled at home. I'd stopped to grab all the dog necessities at the pet supply store. He was taking it all in and was so well-behaved.

I had Oakley in her swing, and Chewy would walk by her, smelling, and then he'd move on. He seemed to be okay around her. I definitely wouldn't leave them alone, but I wasn't too worried either.

"Okay, Chewy, what do you think? You like your new home?"

He wagged his tail and came closer, so I could pet him. He then settled at my feet.

"This isn't going to work for me. I have things to do."

He looked up with his Chewy grin and a wag of his tail. I resolved myself to sit here for at least a few minutes.

A few months ago, I would have called you crazy if you told me I would have a baby and a dog. The baby from my kidnapper and the dog to protect myself from a stalker.

God, my life really was so weird. Maybe I should have that made into a sign to hang on the front door.

Chapter Twenty-Two

"Hey, Joanna?" Tessa said at the door to my office.

"Yeah?"

"Victoria Sellers' family is on the phone. They want to get an appointment with you, and they said they can't wait."

We were booked solid until after our next tour, so it would be easily three or four months before I could see them.

"Did they say why the rush?"

I'm sure I could guess why, and I was positive I would ask her to make it work, even if I had to work outside of my normal hours. If it meant giving them some peace, I would do it.

"They want to thank you for helping find her."

I thought about it for only a split second. I could relate to how they must be feeling, and while they didn't need to thank me, I did want to help them find peace.

"Let's pull up my schedule and see what we can do."

Tessa and I reviewed my appointments and found a slot that I had blocked. It wasn't ideal, but I could make it work, especially if I got the chance to ask them some questions about her and maybe find a connection with her and the other victims. Or perhaps they had some names of potential suspects. Anything to help shed light on this case.

The appointment will be a week from today.

"I hope they don't mind waiting that long," I said before she left.

"I think they'll be happy with it."

We often got special requests, but we didn't always shift things around. This felt like a unique situation, and if I could learn something new for the case, it would be an added bonus.

Tessa returned a few minutes later to let me know they were happy with the appointment time and wanted me to know they appreciated it. I would be glad to help provide them with closure and peace if I could.

A week later, the Sellers had arrived for their appointment. It was her father, mother, and younger sister. They'd brought me a huge flower arrangement as a thank you. I was mildly embarrassed to accept it because I didn't feel I had done much for them.

"Thank you for fitting us in. We know how busy you are." Mr. Sellers said. "We wanted to thank you for your help in finding our Victoria."

His voice caught in his throat. Mrs. Sellers softly sobbed at his side. Ella Sellers reached for her mother's hand.

"I'm sorry I couldn't help more and so sorry for your loss. She seems like such a sweet soul."

"Thanks." Mr. Sellers said. "We're not sure how this works. Do we have to give you information, or do you do something to speak to her?"

"She's actually here with us." They all gasped as I said this, but when they didn't say anything, I continued to explain the process. "You can just speak to her, and I will say what she says as if she is speaking the words. So, if I say 'I' or 'me', it is her saying this."

They nodded but stayed quiet. I looked at Victoria. She was standing by her mother and trying to pat her shoulder, but her hand couldn't connect.

"Victoria, do you have anything you'd like to say?" I said to her.

"I love you all and miss you very much. I hate this happened." She said, and I spoke for her.

"Vicki, we love you too. Life isn't the same without you." Her father choked out.

"I love you, sis." Ella said with tears falling down her face. "But at least I don't have to share the bathroom with you anymore. All the counter space is mine."

Victoria laughed. "Well, enjoy it."

"Is there anything you can tell us about the person who did this to you?" Mr. Sellers asked.

"Not a lot. I caught a glimpse of an older man. Maybe forties or early fifties. He was kind of average height but not really tall." She paused. "He was strong. That's all I can remember, though."

Her mother's weeping grew louder. This was still so fresh for them as it happened just a few weeks ago. I understood the grief and the rawness of the loss.

I passed her the tissue box. She flashed me a sad smile.

"So, no way to tell if he was someone you knew?" Mr. Sellers asked as he twisted a tissue in his hand.

"I definitely didn't know him. His voice was not familiar."

"Why didn't you stay with the group? What have we always told you girls about going out at night?"

"Stay with the group." Both girls said, not realizing they said it together, but when I told Ella, she laughed.

"We were always two peas." She smiled. "That's the hardest part. Losing my best friend."

"I feel the same," Victoria said. She studied her mom for a moment before saying, "Mom, I know this is hard for you. I don't expect you to be okay anytime soon, but please know I will stay nearby for as long as I can, and I'll keep watch over y'all."

The trio broke at the words. I know I could never give it the voice they really needed to hear, but I always tried to give the emotions. It was the best I could do for them, and it seemed to be enough.

"Victoria, do you mind if I ask a few questions about the man?" I asked. She nodded. "You said you caught a glimpse of him. Do you think if you saw him again, you'd recognize him?"

"Honestly, I doubt it. He could be almost anyone. I didn't get a good enough look at his face, but his voice was firm, deep. I think I would recognize that."

"I hate to ask this next question, but were there any signs or threats that you remember before this night? Anyone following you or weird phone calls?"

The group gasped, but I had to ask, especially for my own peace of mind. What if I was a target of the serial killer?

"No, I don't remember anything out of the ordinary before. I had been out with my friends. They went one way, and I went the other. It had been crowded when I arrived, so I had to park further away." She breathed in deeply, then exhaled with a gush. It wasn't true breathing, more of a reaction to her emotions. "I was almost to my car when he grabbed me."

"I'm so sorry." I looked at her family and then back to her. "Did you or do you know any of the other victims?"

"Only now that I'm dead. I hadn't even heard about it before."

"Thanks, and I'm sorry to hijack the reading. I just wanted to see if I could help with the investigation." I looked at her family. "I'm sure y'all have already talked with the police, but just to help me, do you have any information about a possible suspect?"

They all looked at each other. Mrs. Sellers shook her head.

"She was well liked. No weird ex-boyfriends or angry friends." Mrs. Sellers said, speaking for the first time.

"Yeah, no fights with girlfriends or co-workers. Nothing. Nobody." Ella added.

"We've tried, wracking our brains to come up with a name but nothing." Mr. Sellers said.

I nodded, giving a weak smile.

"Well, I'm truly sorry. We still have time if y'all want to continue. I promise I won't ask any more questions."

It took them a moment to get into the rhythm, but they shared one story and then another. Soon even Mrs. Sellers was laughing along with the memories.

It was a good reading, and while I didn't learn anything new about the serial killer, I also knew he hadn't given a warning, so the person who was stalking me had to be a different person. I couldn't decide if that was a comfort or fed my fears, but I was going to hold on to the hope it was a crazed fan.

Chapter Twenty-Three

It sure was an adjustment having a dog. I had to work in his feedings, outside time, and then add in at least one daily walk while pushing a stroller. It was fun, though. I wish I'd done it sooner.

I was just getting back from my morning walk with Chewy when Donovan pulled up. I guess he was going to start the garage today, or I hoped he was.

"Hi, Donovan," I greeted when he hopped out of the van.

"Hi, Joanna." He said. "I hope you don't mind. I wanted to drop off a few things, but I won't be able to start today. I have my mother." He gestured toward the van, and I saw her sitting in the front seat.

I waved to her in the front seat.

She put the window down. "Hi, I'm Mona. Donovan's mom."

Mona had a sweet old lady next door look about her. Her hair was a pale cream color, not gray and not white. She had it braided in a single, thick braid down her back. Her smile was endearing, and you could easily see her offering you a fresh from the oven cookie.

"I'm Joanna. Nice to meet you."

"Nice to meet you as well."

"I was going to start on the garage today, but she's not feeling well, so we are heading to the doctor," Donovan said.

"Oh, I'm sorry to hear. I hope you feel better." I said to Mona.

"Thank you, dear. That's sweet, but when you get to my age, everything falls apart." We chuckled at her joke. "Your daughter is cute."

"Oh, thanks." Chewy was pulling me toward the house. That's weird. He usually liked people. "I better get these two back in the house."

"I'll see you soon, Joanna. Probably tomorrow." Donovan called.

"Sounds good. Again, nice to meet you, Ms. Mona."

"Same to you, dear."

I got the dog and baby back in the house. I put Oakley into her pack-n-play with some toys and got the dog some fresh water.

"What got into you out there, mister?" I asked the dog. "Were you tired from your walk?"

He wagged his tail and grinned at me, then went to lay near Oakley. He loved her.

My dad and Stan were coming over this morning to put in a completely new security system. This one was supposed to be tamper-proof. I sure hope so. I needed an extra level of security.

I called both Micah and Tessa to let them know Donovan was going to start on the garage, and we'd need to move our products. They both agreed they'd be over soon to help move boxes.

I started moving my furniture around to make space for the many boxes, as I waited on everyone to arrive. My dad and Stan were first and were loaded down with tons of equipment.

"Hi, Dad. Stan." I said, opening the door for them. Chewy came wagging his whole butt to greet them.

"Hi, Jo." Dad leaned over and kissed my cheek. "Hi, Chewy. Nice to finally meet you. Now, where is my sweet granddaughter?"

He pushed past me, making a beeline for the living room.

"Hi, Jo," Stan said, bringing up the rear. "Sorry, we have to keep doing this. I hope this time, it takes care of it."

"Me too, but I really appreciate it."

We followed dad into the living room to find he'd put down all his tools and boxes and was playing with Oakley. She cooed and giggled at him.

"She's gotten so big," Dad commented.

"Yes, she has."

"We better get to work," Stan said.

"I'm sorry, little girl, duty calls. Grandpa's gotta help keep his girls safe." He looked over and winked at me. I had the best dad.

"Thanks, Dad."

They got to work taking out the old system first. That took them a while. In between my own project, I checked in with them here and there, bringing them drinks or handing tools.

Micah arrived with his boyfriend, Josh, in tow.

"I figured we could use the extra hands, boss."

"Always. Happy to see you again, Josh." I said, hugging him.

"I just came to see the little miss. Where is that sweet baby?" Josh walked over and scooped her up.

Micah rolled his eyes, and I laughed. Josh was ready for kids, while Micah was still enjoying being free and sleeping in.

When Tessa arrived, we got right to work. We had a lot of products to move and not enough space in my house for it.

Around lunchtime, I ordered some Chinese takeout. It arrived along with Clint.

"Hey, nice surprise. What are you doing here?" I said when I opened the door to find him and the delivery guy standing at the door.

"I brought Chinese." The delivery driver said.

"Yes, thank you. And you?" I looked at Clint.

"I smelled the food." He joked. "But seriously, you had mentioned your dad and Stan were working on the security system, so I came by to see if they needed help."

"That's sweet. I'm sure they will take all the help they can get. Plus, the rest of us are moving boxes. We have enough work that we could use the extra hands." I signed the slip for the food. "Thank you."

He nodded and left while Clint followed me and the food into the kitchen.

"You're lucky. I ordered extras." I teased him.

"I've always had good luck like that." He winked.

"Let me go call them for lunch. They're up in the attic at the moment." I started to walk away. "Help yourself to a drink."

"Thanks."

I called up into the attic and got an immediate response. I knew they'd be hungry.

"Hey, detective." My dad said when he came into the room.

"Hi, Mr. Webber."

"Please, call me Charlie."

"Okay. I thought I'd offer my services. I've done a little of this type of work before." Clint said.

"Happy to have the help, but first lunch," Dad said as he washed his hands.

Clint greeted the others. Micah and I pulled out all the food while Josh got plates, and Tessa got drinks for everyone. Then we all filled our plates and sat around the table.

As we ate, there was small talk among everyone, but mostly the guys. Tessa and I were observers. It was nice to see some of my favorite men bonding over sports and food. Oakley was in her swing nearby and was "talking" along with everyone, always wanting to be part of the conversation.

Chewy was under the table hoping for a dropped morsel or handout.

After the meal was eaten and the mess cleaned up, I received a thank you from everyone.

"I need to drop by more often. That was good." Clint whispered for only my ears.

Everyone else got back to work while I dealt with getting Oakley fed, then changed and down for a nap.

Once she was down, I helped finish up moving the products from the garage to the house. My house was going to look like a hoarder situation for a week or so, but I had hoped the end product would be amazing.

"Well, boss, that's the last of it," Micah said as he set the last box down.

"Wow. This is more than I thought."

"You're popular."

"I guess." I laughed.

"Sorry to run out on you, but Josh and I need to get going. Engagement party for some friends over in Buckston."

"Have fun and thanks."

"I have to run too," Tessa said. "Babysitting for my cousin."

I walked them all out but then didn't know what to do with myself. At times, I hated my non-workdays because I didn't have hobbies to keep me busy. My work was my hobby.

I wonder if I should be doing some investigation on the Playhouse Killer. I was smart, but I had to be missing a clue to how these ladies were connected.

So far, other than looks, two of them had been dating guys that worked for Hank with one of those working at his hangout, Leo's. Could that be the connection?

I decided to go dig into both Darius and Matt's backgrounds a bit. Hours later, I was frustrated because I kept hitting blank walls. I guess working for Hank meant having almost no online footprint. Though I did see some evidence of life on their respective girlfriend's social media. It had been enough to identify them when I met Darius and Matt, but not much else.

I decided to look into Hank and Al and a few others that I knew worked for Hank. It was mostly my curiosity. The only things I found were news stories that mentioned Hank here and there. Nothing personal on any of them. He did a lot of goodwill and charity for the town in addition to his other business activities.

"Huh, that's interesting," I said out loud.

"Talking to yourself?" Clint said as he stepped into my office. I jumped nearly out of my skin. "Oh, I'm sorry. I didn't mean to startle you."

"I was doing some research. I guess I was so focused I didn't hear you."

"I understand. What were you researching?"

"Hank."

"Why?" Clint asked, taking a seat across from me.

"I was trying to determine a connection with the killer's victims. The only thing I could come up with was that two of them were dating guys that worked for Hank." I dropped my hands into my lap. "I know it's likely random, but I thought it was worth a look."

"Yeah, definitely worth a look. So, did you find anything?"

"Nope. I see why you're so frustrated with this case. There's nothing."

"Yeah, nothing. This guy is good at covering his tracks."

"But that's not why you came in here?" I said smiling flirtatiously.

"Right. Just wanted to say goodbye. Working the evening shift." He said. "Your Dad and Stan are nearly finished with the security system, so I figured I could leave them."

I nodded as I stood, then walked around the desk so I could walk him out. Instead of making a move to leave, he pulled me to him, hugging me tightly. We didn't say anything for a few seconds, just enjoyed the shared moment.

I finally said, "Thanks for coming. I appreciate the help, and I'm sure they were happy for the extra hands."

"I was happy to help, plus I got to see you." He smiled at me. "I'll see you again soon."

He kissed me lightly and then stepped back with a smile.

"I'll walk you out," I said weakly.

Chapter Twenty-Four

~Stalker~

So, they think a new security system is going to stop me? No way. If I wanted to get her, I would. The timing isn't right yet, but soon. Very soon.

But what got my blood boiling was that she let that detective in again. What could she possibly see in him? He was a dud. He was such a by-the-book type guy that he had to be boring.

She just didn't know enough about me. I'd have to send her some clues, and maybe she'd understand why she had to dump the detective and go for me.

I paced in my room while I tried to come up with an idea. It had to be good. Not something violent or mean. I'd never hurt her. The other girls, sure, but not her.

She hadn't reacted to the graffiti the way I'd expected. She simply had it fixed and moved on with her day.

Her strength and resilience were things I admired about her, but I'd wanted fear to drive her to me. Unfortunately, I'd underestimated her.

Though if I were honest with myself, I'd admit that she barely knew I existed. I'd have to change that.

A few ideas were coming together, and I had the time to make it right. I couldn't scare her further into his arms. That was not the goal.

No, no, that would never do.

It had to be just the right thing while I put the finishing touches on my ultimate goal. Then we'd be together away from everything and everyone.

As I paced, Mother bellowed for me, causing me to groan internally. She was so needy. I balled my fists as a thought formed.

I wish I had the guts to end her life. She always interrupted my time. I left my sanctuary to go see what she wanted now.

Chapter Twenty-Five

The next morning, I was taking the trash out to the curb when I noticed a dark gray car driving slowly toward me.

"Hey, Joanna!" The familiar voice called from inside the car.

"Oh, hi, Fabio." I settled the trash can in place. "What are y'all doing here?"

I was suddenly aware of how rough I looked. I'd thrown some clothes on when Oakley cried this morning and hadn't bothered with a bra or fixing my hair. At the thought of Fabio seeing me braless, I crossed my arms over my chest.

"Heading to my friend's house. The one I told y'all about that lives nearby. Then I have dogs to walk."

"Wow, okay. I just keep seeing you around. I didn't realize how much our paths crossed."

"Oh yeah, it's funny." He chuckled. "I didn't realize you lived here until I came to audition that day, but I have been spending more time in this area lately." He looked straight ahead for a moment, then back. "My previous job was different. I was locked inside all day. I like this, being out and about."

I nodded. I hadn't considered what he'd done before magic. His tense body language suggested it was something he hadn't enjoyed or had caused him stress. Maybe both.

Since I'd let Micah take the lead on this, I hadn't done my typical research. Maybe I should have done at least a bit. This required a conversation with Micah to get some additional information on Fabio or his thoughts on why I was running into him everywhere.

"Well, I better get back inside. Take care." I waved while trying to keep my chest covered and turned without waiting for his reply. Though I did hear him say something as I walked away.

When I got back in the house, I was greeted by the smiling face and wagging tail of my new dog and a sick feeling about the man we recently hired to be our opening act. What if he was the killer? He kept showing up everywhere I was.

I peeked in on the baby. She was down for her morning nap and safe in her room.

Back in the office, Micah was working on tour details. He looked up when I walked in.

"Morning, boss."

"Morning." I sat down at my desk. "Can I ask you something about Fabio?"

"Sure, what's up?"

"How much do you know about him? I mean, did you do a background check or anything?"

Micah leaned back in his chair. "I did the standard stuff. No criminal record, good references from Barkers. Why? Is something wrong?"

"I don't know. Maybe I'm being paranoid, but I keep running into him everywhere. Just now, he was driving by my house."

"He did mention he has a friend nearby and walks dogs in this area."

"Yeah, he said that. It's probably nothing." I fidgeted with a pen on my desk.

"Boss, if you're uncomfortable, we can look deeper into his background. Or we could reconsider hiring him."

"No, no. I'm probably just on edge with everything going on. The murders, the break-in, all of it. I'm seeing threats where there might not be any."

"That's understandable. Y'all have been through a lot." Micah said. "But trust your instincts. If something feels off, it probably is."

I thought about that. My instincts had been wrong before, but they'd also saved me. The problem was knowing which was which.

"Let me think about it. For now, let's just keep moving forward with the tour plans."

"You got it." Micah turned back to his computer.

I tried to focus on work, but my mind kept drifting back to Fabio standing across the street, to all the times I'd randomly seen him. Coincidence? Or something more sinister?

The thought made me check the baby monitor again. Oakley was still sleeping peacefully.

I pulled up my calendar and started reviewing the week's appointments, but concentration eluded me. Every car that passed outside made me look up. Every creak of the house settling made me tense.

"Gawd, I'm a mess," I muttered to myself.

"What was that?" Micah asked.

"Nothing. Just talking to myself."

Maybe I should call Clint. But what would I say? That my new employee drives through my neighborhood? That seemed ridiculous. I needed something more concrete before making accusations.

For now, I'd just stay vigilant and keep my eyes open. If Fabio really was involved in something sinister, he'd slip up eventually. They always did.

At least, I hoped that was true.

Chapter Twenty-Six

~Clint~

I stared at the autopsy report for Macy, frustration building with every line I read. Just like the others, there was no strange DNA. Rope burns on her ankles and wrists, but not much to indicate a struggle beyond that. And then, of course, the stab wounds.

The toxicology showed diazepam, same as the others. Not enough to kill her, but likely enough to keep her dazed while he did his work. The multiple stab wounds and blood loss had killed her.

The only silver lining in this whole mess was that he hadn't sexually assaulted any of them. It wasn't much comfort, but at least it was one less horror they'd endured.

And if this was the same person stalking Jo, I had to catch him before something happened to her. Or rather, before something else happened. I still hadn't figured out who locked her and Micah in that building by the airport. When Terry and I interviewed people around there, they'd all talked about a van, not a car.

A green sedan wasn't much to go on. And it wasn't even a reliable witness, since it came from someone I couldn't question directly. I had to depend on Joanna to talk to her ghost, and I still wasn't sure I believed any of it was real.

But whether I believed it or not, Jo needed to be more careful. She needed to stop trying to take matters into her own hands. If only I could keep her from pulling these idiotic stunts. There was a real threat out there, and I didn't need her putting herself in harm's way like she kept doing.

The thought of that double date with her sister and brother-in-law made me smile despite the grim report in front of me. She'd looked gorgeous in that flowy dress. It had hugged her curves just right. We'd had a great dinner, and I'd enjoyed getting to know Stan and Audrey as much as I was getting to know Joanna. I'd been spending more and more time with her lately.

And I liked it. A lot.

"What are y'all smiling about?" Terry's voice cut through my thoughts.

I looked up, clearing the smile off my face. "Nothing."

"If you say so." He leaned against the doorframe, arms crossed.

"What's up?"

"I was coming to see about that report." He gestured toward the file on my desk.

We were still old school here at the precinct. Some things had moved to electronic files, but reports like this were still better the traditional way.

"You can have it. I'm not seeing anything new." I handed it over.

Terry took the seat across from my desk and flipped through the report without a word. The silence stretched between us, broken only by the rustle of paper.

"This is frustrating," he finally said. "This guy is good. Too good."

"Yeah." I leaned back in my chair. "Between you and me, I'm not feeling confident in my skills anymore. Not after the Landon case."

"True. Me neither." Terry closed the file. "But who would've suspected Cate? The toy poodle?"

I nodded. We'd all called her that because she'd always been perfectly polished and groomed, like a show dog. Now that she was in jail, she couldn't color her hair or get her nails done like before. The nickname didn't quite fit anymore.

"She fooled us all," I said. "Made me question everything I thought I knew about reading people."

"Same. And now we've got this guy who's even better at hiding." Terry tapped the file. "No witnesses, no DNA, nothing that leads anywhere."

"There's got to be something we're missing." I rubbed my eyes. I'd been staring at reports for hours. "Some connection between the victims we haven't found yet."

"Jo find anything useful when she talked to them?"

I shook my head. "Not much. They didn't see him clearly. He drugged them fast, kept them dazed. They remember pain and fear but not details that help us."

"Figures." Terry stood, tucking the file under his arm. "I'll take another look at this, see if fresh eyes catch something."

"Thanks."

He paused at the door. "You serious about Jo? Not just, you know, grateful she helped us with Cate?"

The question caught me off guard. Was I serious about her? The answer should've been simple, but nothing about Joanna Webber was simple.

"I don't know," I admitted. "Maybe. She's different from anyone I've dated before."

"Different how?"

"She's stubborn, reckless, drives me crazy half the time." I smiled despite myself. "But she's also brave and caring, and when she sets her mind to something, nothing stops her."

"Sounds like you got it bad, partner."

"Maybe I do."

After Terry left, I turned back to the case files spread across my desk. Somewhere in all this paperwork was the answer. A pattern, a clue, something that would lead us to this killer before he struck again.

Before he decided Jo looked too much like his type and made her his next victim.

That thought made my stomach turn. I picked up my phone and texted her.

Everything okay there?

The reply came fast. **Yes. Why?**

Just checking. Stay safe.

Always do.

I smiled at that lie. Joanna Webber didn't know the meaning of staying safe. But gawd help me, I was falling for her anyway.

Chapter Twenty-Seven

~Joanna~

It had been a few days since Donovan started the work in the garage, and my house was still full of Medium with a Heart merchandise. Box after box of our various products. My kitchen table had become our packing area, littered with tape dispensers, shipping labels, and bubble wrap.

I was thankful Oakley couldn't crawl yet, though she could scoot now. More of a roll and kick than actual scooting. She'd be four months soon, so I knew my days of keeping her in one spot were numbered.

While Oakley was still asleep and before Donovan arrived, I went to peek at the work he'd gotten done the day before.

The smell of fresh wood welcomed me when I stepped into the garage. He'd nearly finished building one row of shelves, and the packing area had been framed out. Boards for it were already cut and leaning against the wall.

"Wow," I said to the empty space.

I could picture it all. Rows of product, organized on each shelf. A shipping area with all the tools needed to get merchandise to our customers. It was going to transform how we ran the business.

I was walking out of the garage just as Donovan came up the driveway.

"Good morning." He smiled and waved.

"Oh, good morning, Donovan." I jumped, not having heard him pull up, then blushed with embarrassment. "Sorry, I was checking out your work. It looks great."

"I'm glad y'all like it."

"I do. You got so much done already. Impressive."

"Thanks. Yeah, I should knock out the packing area and that row of shelves today, then start on the next row."

"Wow. That'll be great." I started backing toward the house. "Well, I better head back in and get ready for work too. Have a good one."

"You too, Jo." He smiled as I walked away.

I went back inside, side-stepping around piles of inventory to get to my office. I had a full day of readings, and we were just over a month away from the tour. Emails to check. Travel plans to review. The usual chaos of running a business while pretending to talk to the dead.

When my first client showed up, it hit me how distracting the garage work would be during readings. I hadn't had any clients the last few days, so I hadn't thought about it.

"I'm so sorry about the noise. I'm having some work done in the garage." I said to the Blakes when I noticed Mrs. Blake shifting uncomfortably and making disgusted faces over her shoulder toward the sound of hammering.

"It's fine. As long as we get our full time." Her tone was sharp.

"Of course."

I went back to translating what her late husband allegedly had to say. He was sharing a memory of their honeymoon. They'd taken a dream trip to Greece, and he got food poisoning, but it brought them closer as a couple.

"And after my second-guessing about getting married so young, that moment was when I knew for sure I'd made the right choice. I had found my one true love." I delivered the line with as much emotion as I could muster.

"Me too, Quincy. Me too." Mrs. Blake dabbed at her eyes with a tissue.

The rest of the reading went smoothly, despite occasional banging from the garage. When they left, Mrs. Blake seemed satisfied, clutching the recording of our session like it was precious cargo.

I had a fifteen-minute break before my next client. I grabbed some water and checked on Oakley, who was happily batting at the toys hanging from her play gym.

"Having fun, baby girl?" I leaned down and kissed her forehead.

She cooed in response, and I felt that familiar surge of love mixed with terror. How was I supposed to keep this tiny human safe when I kept finding myself tangled up in murder investigations?

My phone buzzed. A text from Clint.

Everything okay there?

I smiled at the screen. He'd been checking in more frequently since the break-in.

Yes. Why?

Just checking. Stay safe.

Always do.

I typed the lie easily enough. Staying safe wasn't exactly my strong suit.

The doorbell rang, announcing my next client. I glanced at my calendar. The Martins. Their teenage son had died in a car accident six months ago. This was going to be an emotional one.

I took a deep breath, pushed thoughts of Clint and serial killers and construction noise out of my mind, and went to answer the door.

Time to put on the show.

By the time my last reading ended around four, I was exhausted. The emotional weight of grieving families, combined with the constant hammering from the garage, had left me drained.

I found Donovan packing up his tools.

"How'd it go today?" I asked.

"Great. Got the packing area done and started on the second row of shelves. Should have everything finished by the end of the week."

"That's amazing. Thank y'all so much."

"Happy to help." He loaded the last of his tools into his truck. "See you tomorrow, Jo."

After he left, I stood in the garage, admiring the progress. It really was going to be perfect for our needs. Maybe hiring him had been one of my better decisions.

Though I couldn't shake the nagging feeling that something about all of this felt off. Fabio showing up everywhere. Donovan working in my garage. The murders. Clint's growing concern.

Maybe I was just paranoid. Or maybe my instincts were trying to tell me something.

I locked the garage door and went back inside to feed Oakley and try to forget, for just a little while, that there was a killer out there who liked women who looked just like me.

Chapter Twenty-Eight

"Thanks, guys." I handed Oakley to Josh, who immediately started making silly faces at her. "I really appreciate y'all doing this."

"No problem at all. This will give us good practice for when we have kids." Josh gushed, bouncing her gently.

"Babe," Micah said, but there was a slight twinkle in his eye.

"You know you want kids, babe."

"Y'all would be great dads." I grabbed my purse and checked my reflection one more time in the hallway mirror.

Oakley cooed and laughed, grabbing Josh's face with her tiny hands.

"Oh, aren't you just the cutest little bug." Josh planted a kiss on her forehead.

Chewy was seated at Micah's feet, tail thumping against the floor. They were best buds. During the workday, Chewy spent most of his time following Micah around since I had to keep him out of my office during client sessions. Never knew who had allergies or who was scared of large dogs.

There was a knock at the door. Chewy jumped up and ran for it, barking and tail wagging like a helicopter.

"Must be Clint." I kissed Oakley's head. "Have fun, guys. She should go down around eight."

I opened the door with a smile. Clint looked handsome in his usual polo and jeans with those worn brown boots. Simple, but it worked for him.

"Hi." He said as I stepped out the door.

"Hi yourself."

"All good?" He nodded toward the house.

"Yep, she's in good hands."

"Great."

He opened the truck door, holding my hand as I climbed into the cab. I practically had to hop up to get in. Clint was tall, so it was easy for him. Me? Not so much.

"You still good with eating at Quench?" He asked as he started the truck.

"Yep, sounds good."

I'd learned it was his favorite place. He went there a lot, apparently. I didn't have a strong opinion about it. The food was decent enough, and I didn't have a better suggestion.

We drove over, chatting about nothing in particular. Just day-to-day stuff. The one thing we didn't mention was the Playhouse Killer. It was nice to pretend, for a little while, that my life was normal.

Quench was packed as usual, but he'd made reservations, so we didn't have to wait long.

As we walked to our table, I noticed a familiar face. Fabio, sitting with an older woman. When he saw me, his eyes widened with what looked like genuine surprise.

He mouthed an apology as we turned just before passing him. I mouthed back that it was fine. His companion glared at me over her shoulder. Definitely his mother, based on that look.

We got seated and reviewed the menu. The waitress took our drink order and told us about their specials. Once she returned with our drinks, we were ready to order.

"Sounds good. It'll be out shortly." She tapped her pen on the pad before walking away.

"I'm glad we could go out again." Clint said once we were alone.

"Me too." I smiled. "Weird to see Fabio here, though. He seems to be everywhere I go lately."

"Huh. Weird." Clint looked around, but we were seated in a different section without a direct view of where Fabio sat. "Are you worried?"

Did I sound worried? I hoped not. I didn't want to cause trouble where my paranoid brain was projecting it.

"No, not at all. It's just strange how I never knew him before, but now he's all over the place. Makes you wonder how many times I'd been places he was and never knew. How many other people here might be part of my life in the future, and I don't know yet?"

"Dang, Jo, that's getting deep." He laughed.

"Ha, yeah, a bit. Sorry." I flashed him a sheepish grin. "So how are, um, sports?"

I knew nothing about sports. Wasn't even sure what season it was. My understanding of different seasons came from Bugs Bunny fighting with Daffy Duck about whether it was duck season or rabbit season.

"Sports are good." He chuckled, clearly amused by my attempt. "How are baby things?"

"You're funny. Baby things are good. She's growing so fast. I swear she does something new every day."

We continued chatting while waiting for our food. Clint told me about baseball season, and I told him about what a nearly four-month-old baby should be doing. Not exactly riveting conversation, but it was comfortable. Easy.

The waitress checked on us a few times before bringing our meals.

"Looks good." Clint said as she set down our plates. "Thanks, Krista."

He knew everyone here. Clearly, he'd been here a time or two. Or a million. For myself, I'd only been a few times.

We were halfway through our meal when I saw Fabio approaching our table. My stomach tightened.

"Um, Joanna, sorry to bother y'all." He said nervously. "I wanted to apologize in person. I didn't know you'd be here. I swear I'm not following you." He laughed, but it sounded forced.

"Oh, it's fine. I didn't think you were."

Clint's eyes narrowed as he looked at Fabio, then back at me.

"It's just after Micah talked to me, I realized how odd this all must seem. It's funny we always end up in the same places. Like now." He fidgeted with his hands. "Here I was taking my mom out for a special dinner, and then here you are."

"Oh, that's nice to take her out. Y'all have a good relationship?" I was right about it being his mother.

"Yeah, not always great. She was disappointed in my choice of careers. Who wants a magician for a son?" He laughed again, more naturally this time. "Well, maybe some people, I suppose."

"I understand that." My own mother hated what I did.

"That was it. Just wanted y'all to know I'm not some creep." He smiled. "Take care."

He hurried back to the other section of the restaurant and to his mother, who was watching us with a sour expression.

That was actually kind of sweet that he took her out. Anyone who had a nice relationship with their mother couldn't be a killer, right? Then again, Ted Bundy probably took his mother out to dinner too.

"What the heck was that about?" Clint asked once Fabio was out of earshot.

"I told you. It's been strange. He's everywhere."

Clint studied me. I tried to keep my face neutral and not fidget under his scrutiny. He finally went back to his dinner, but I could tell he was processing what just happened.

We completed our meal without any other uncomfortable visitors or odd conversations. Made it to our movie with plenty of time, and the rest of the evening was blessedly predictable.

No strange cars following us. No break-ins waiting at home. No ghostly victims asking me to track down their bodies.

Just a normal date. Novel concept.

"Do you want to come in while I relieve Micah and Josh?" I asked when we pulled up at my house.

"Sure."

I unlocked the door and was greeted by Chewy's enthusiastic welcome. He whined and wagged his whole body like I'd been gone for weeks instead of hours.

"Hey, Chewy. Did you miss me?" I rubbed his head and scratched behind his ears.

"Oh, hey, boss," Micah said, coming into the foyer. "Hey, Clint."

"Hey," Clint replied.

"No problems, I assume?"

"She was wonderful. A perfect little angel." Josh said, joining us with a sleeping Oakley in his arms.

"She's all tucked in bed. Clean and fed." Micah told me.

"Great. I appreciate y'all watching her."

I kissed them each on the cheek, and we all said goodbyes. Once they left, the house felt suddenly quiet. Just me and Clint and the soft sound of Oakley's breathing through the baby monitor.

"Want a drink?" I offered.

"Um, sure."

"Are you sure?" I teased at his hesitation.

"Yeah, yeah. I was thinking I should go, but there's no reason to rush." He smiled and pulled me closer.

I looked up at him. He leaned down and kissed me. Not the soft, sweet kisses we'd shared before. This was more passionate. Hungrier.

I met his passion, enjoying the feel of his lips. They were soft yet firm, and gawd, the man could kiss.

"Nice," he whispered as the kiss ended. "I'd been thinking about that all evening."

"Me too," I admitted.

Hours later, I was walking him out. We'd talked about everything and nothing, sitting on the couch with our drinks, stealing kisses between conversations.

"Good night, Jo." He said against my lips as we shared one last kiss before he left.

"Good night, Clint."

I watched his taillights disappear down the street, then locked up and checked all the windows. Old habits.

My phone buzzed as I was getting ready for bed. A text from Clint.

Made it home safe. Sleep well.

I smiled at the screen.

You too. Thanks for tonight.

Anytime.

I plugged in my phone and climbed into bed, but sleep didn't come easily. My mind kept replaying the evening. The date had been nice. Really nice. But Fabio showing up, again, gnawed at me.

Coincidence? Probably.

But in my experience, there were no coincidences when it came to murder.

Chapter Twenty-Nine

~Joanna~

"That's our time for today." I said to my current clients, the Suttons. "I think this was a great reading."

"Yes, thank you so much. This helps give me comfort." Mrs. Sutton said, holding her young son close.

Her husband had passed away from cancer not long after their son was born. Now, two years later, Mrs. Sutton was ready to reach out and share all about their little boy. Her husband had assured her through me that he was close by, watching. He'd seen the first steps and heard his first words.

"That makes me so happy. I thought you would miss it all." She gazed down at her son with tears in her eyes.

I walked her out.

"Can I hug you?" She asked at the door.

"Of course."

We hugged. Her son wiggled and giggled in her arms, reaching out to pat my face with his tiny hand.

"Thanks for this. It really makes me feel less alone and not as sad that he missed out."

"I'm happy we were able to talk to him today."

I watched as she buckled her son into his car seat, then waved as she drove away. I stood for a moment, watching her car disappear around the corner.

That was a nice reading. One of the reasons I kept doing this, despite the guilt of the lie. If I could give people peace, maybe it balanced out the deception.

Back in the office, I got on my computer. After checking my schedule and emails, I clicked on the local news station's website. We'd had a lot of rain recently, and I wanted to see if I'd be able to take Oakley and Chewy to the park later.

A headline caught my eye. It was about the serial killer's victims.

I clicked on the article, my stomach tightening as I read. They'd updated the victim count. Eight now. Eight women who looked eerily similar to each other.

And to me.

The article included photos of all the victims together in a collage. Dark hair, dark eyes, similar heights and builds. My hands trembled slightly as I stared at the screen.

I pulled up my own publicity photo in another tab and placed it next to the victims' photos. The similarities were undeniable. Not identical, but close enough to make my skin crawl.

"Gawd," I whispered.

My phone buzzed. A text from Clint.

Did you see the news?

Yes. Just now.

Stay inside today. I'm serious, Jo.

I wanted to argue, to tell him I couldn't live my life in fear. But looking at those photos, fear seemed like the appropriate response.

Okay.

I'll check in later.

I closed the browser tabs, but the images were burned into my mind. Eight women. Eight families destroyed. And whoever was doing this had a very specific type.

Oakley's cry came through the baby monitor, pulling me from my dark thoughts. I pushed away from the desk and went to get her.

"Hey, baby girl," I said softly, lifting her from the crib. "You hungry?"

She gurgled in response, her little fist finding its way to her mouth.

I carried her to the kitchen, bouncing her gently as I prepared her bottle with one hand. It was a skill I'd perfected over the last few months. The whole one-handed-parenting thing.

While she ate, I stared out the kitchen window. Donovan's van was in the driveway. I'd completely forgotten he was working in the garage today. The sound of hammering had become white noise.

Through the window, I could see him moving around in the garage. He seemed focused on his work, measuring something against the wall.

My phone buzzed again. This time it was a call from an unknown number. I hesitated, then answered.

"Hello?"

Silence.

"Hello?" I said again.

Still nothing. Just the faint sound of breathing.

My heart rate picked up. "Who is this?"

The line went dead.

I stared at the phone, my hand shaking. Wrong number? Or something more sinister?

Oakley finished her bottle and let out a satisfied burp. I forced a smile and kissed her forehead.

"You're so easy to please," I told her. "Bottle, clean diaper, and you're happy."

I carried her to the living room and set her in her play gym. Chewy immediately came over to lie next to her, his tail thumping against the floor. Good dog. Protective dog.

I grabbed my phone and pulled up Clint's number. My thumb hovered over the call button. Should I tell him about the silent call? It could be nothing. A wrong number. A butt dial.

But with everything going on, it felt like something.

Before I could decide, there was a knock at my office door. I jumped, my heart racing.

"Joanna? It's Donovan. Got a question about the shelving."

I exhaled slowly. "Just a minute."

I checked on Oakley one more time, then went to answer the door.

Donovan stood there with his measuring tape, looking perfectly normal. Perfectly harmless.

"Sorry to bother y'all," he said. "Just wanted to confirm the height you want for the top shelf."

"Um, let me come look."

I followed him out to the garage, keeping my phone in my pocket. The space was really coming together. Two full rows of shelves stood completed, and he was working on the third.

"This is amazing," I said, meaning it.

"Thanks. So, the height?" He gestured to the wall.

We discussed the measurements, and I gave him my preferences. He nodded, making notes on a small pad he pulled from his pocket.

"Should have this done by end of week," he said.

"That's great. Thank y'all so much."

He smiled and went back to work. I returned to the house, locking the door behind me.

The rest of the afternoon passed without incident. No more strange calls. No more headlines about murdered women. Just me, Oakley, and Chewy in our little bubble of normalcy.

But I couldn't shake the feeling that the bubble was getting thinner. More fragile.

And sooner or later, it was going to pop.

Chapter Thirty

Shortly before my second appointment of the day, Emma appeared. The second victim I'd spoken to.

"Hi, Joanna the Medium. Bet you didn't think you'd see me again." She said in her bubbly voice.

"Hey, Emma. No, I didn't. Do you have information about the killer?"

"Nah, nothing new. I have talked with a few of the others, so that's been interesting. We all remember more or less the same things."

"So I've noticed. Then if not here for that, what's up?"

"You have an appointment with my sister, Zoe."

"Oh, this is your sister. I didn't know."

"Yeah, she wants to know if I'm haunting her." She giggled. "Of course I am. I told y'all about that a little. It's so fun."

There was a knock at the door. I had to guess that was her. I went to open it.

"Hi, welcome. Are you Zoe?"

"I am."

I gestured for her to come in. "Here, let's go to my office. Would y'all like a drink? Water, tea, coffee?"

"Water would be nice. Thank you." She looked around before taking a seat on the edge of one of my high-back chairs. It was where most people sat, but her body language made me look twice.

She kept looking around with wide eyes, anxious. Like she'd seen a ghost. I wanted to giggle and get caught up in Emma's excitement, but it was unprofessional, and poor Zoe looked like a mess.

I went to the kitchen, grabbing a bottle of water. When I came back into the room, I saw she'd grabbed a few tissues and was twisting them in her hands.

"I'm sorry I helped myself." She held up the tissues.

"Oh, that's fine. That's what they're for." I handed her the water.

She mumbled a thank you.

"Before we get started, I'll first tell you about my process. I'll speak as if I am your sister. You can talk as if directly to her—"

"Wait, you already know why I'm here? I never told y'all that." Tears sprang to her eyes. "I thought I might have to say more."

"No, I've spoken with Emma before, and she's here now."

Zoe started sobbing harder. I handed her the whole box of tissues, knowing those few in her hand wouldn't last long.

"I'm so sorry, Em. I know I shouldn't have slept with Chris. We didn't mean for it to go that way, but we're in love."

"In love? Ha. Neither of you knows what love is. You're both a couple of narcissistic losers."

"Emma, please. I know you're still angry, but please stop haunting us. I know it's you."

"Of course it's me, and as long as I can stay on Earth, I'm going to haunt y'all."

"Fine, be mad. It isn't like we were ever close. Just two strangers that happened to have the same parents." Zoe said. "Have y'all seen mom and dad in the afterlife?"

"No, thank goodness. I would have some words for them too."

Poor Emma. She seemed so angry at her family, the people she should be close to. But I understood how families could be dysfunctional. I might be close to my sister and my dad, but my mother was a whole other story.

"I'm sorry to both of y'all. This sounds like such a tough issue between you." I said as myself.

The sisters both stared at me.

"Joanna's right, Emma. This is a tough issue, and it goes deeper than a boyfriend. We never properly mourned our parents or even our childhood. Bouncing around between relatives."

"I don't care about that. I'm dead now and don't have to worry about any of it anymore."

"Emma—"

"No, Zoe. I'm not listening to you anymore."

Zoe sat quietly weeping, head bent, pressing tissue after tissue to her eyes.

"Fine, Zoe. I'll stop haunting y'all, at least as much."

"I'll take what I can get. I just hope you find it in your heart to forgive me one day." She wiped her nose. "For what it's worth, I'm sorry you were killed."

"Whatever... um, thanks." Emma appeared to put on a brave face, but that last part seemed to catch her off guard.

I watched as she reached forward toward her sister, but before she touched her—well, a ghost touch—she pulled her hand back and crossed her arms over her chest.

We wrapped up, and Zoe left, but Emma stayed behind.

"I'm so sorry for that. I know it isn't your usual style of readings. You like to give closure and happiness. All rainbows and lollipops." She looked out the window. "That will never happen between us. We had drug-abusing parents and got bounced around between them and various relatives, until one day they overdosed."

"That's tough. I'm sorry."

"Meh, it's okay. Like I told you before, I'm fine with this. It beats my life."

I nodded because I had no idea what to say.

"I really appreciate your time and even more, trying to find the killer. I'll be seeing ya." With that, she left.

I had to take a break after that reading. The anger and drama of it hurt my heart. Janie had Oakley here today, so I went for some baby snuggles.

Chewy left Micah's side long enough to come visit me too. I gave him a good all-over scratch. He loved it and bounced around me for more.

"You are good for my soul, Chewy."

After I got recharged by seeing my daughter and dog, I was ready for the rest of the day. My next client was much more loving and fun. It was a family who wanted to connect with their father. His wife and three adult children. They joked through the whole reading and made it enjoyable.

It was after their appointment that I realized there wasn't any construction noise coming from my garage. I grabbed Chewy and went to check on the progress. I knew he was close to being done. Maybe he finally was.

Stepping outside, I saw a pile of leftover lumber and other construction debris, but no sign of Donovan. I opened the garage to find it was all done.

"Wow, Chewy, look at this." It was gorgeous. He'd painted all the shelves a light gray color. "This looks amazing and is going to help so much."

I turned to leave and noticed a note taped by the door. It was from Donovan.

Hi Joanna,

As you can see, I'm finished. Let the paint dry for 48 hours before filling the shelves.

I'll be by in a few days to get the leftovers out of your way. I hope you like the work.

How nice of him to leave a note. I'd be sure to leave a positive review for him online, so hopefully it helped his business. I let Chewy into the backyard to run around.

It was time for Janie to leave, so I needed to get Oakley from her. Then I went to let both Micah and Tessa know we could start moving into the garage in a few days.

"Alright, boss, I'll organize a few people to help us. Good?" Micah said.

"Yes, thanks. It'll be nice to have my house back to normal, and just in time. This little one is dying to crawl. Did I tell y'all she's getting up on her knees already?"

"No, she's too young." Tessa said with a laugh.

"I know. I tried to tell her." I chuckled. "She didn't listen."

Tessa put her arms out to the baby, who went right to her, grabbing her face and slobbering all over her cheek. "You're growing too fast, little girl. I still can't believe you adopted her."

"I know. It's been scary and amazing."

"I didn't think you liked kids." Tessa teased.

"I like kids." I laughed, then changed the subject. "Do y'all want to see the garage?"

They agreed, and we headed out to look at the work.

"He did a great job, boss." Micah said as he stood by the packing area. "This area alone is going to be a game-changer. There's so much space and a place for scissors, box cutters, and all the tape."

"You picked the right guy, Jo."

"I think so too."

We planned where all the different products would go and how we would organize everything. Once we had a game plan, they went back inside and wrapped up work for the day.

After they left, it was just me, the baby, and the dog.

"What shall we do tonight?" I asked the pair.

Oakley giggled.

Chewy wagged his tail.

"To the park it is."

I put her in the stroller, hooked the leash on Chewy, and away we went. I loved my neighborhood. We had a beautiful park at the end of my street with benches, picnic tables, and a large playground area.

Oakley and Chewy both liked to watch the neighborhood children running around, laughing, and playing. They often came over to say hello to both baby and dog.

There was also a baby swing that Oakley had just gotten old enough to sit in and hold her head up enough for. She would giggle as I softly pushed her, the swing just barely moving, but it was enough.

All the recent stress was soon forgotten in this small moment of joy with my daughter and dog.

Chapter Thirty-One

A few days later, I woke up early, anxious to get my house in order. Oakley was getting more mobile each day. I didn't know what she was in such a hurry to grow up for, but I needed the floor space to let her figure it out.

I went out to the garage to check the paint. It felt completely dry. Happy dance. I went back into the house to start my morning routine and wait for my employees to arrive so we could begin cleaning out my house.

We had a small army of Micah's friends join us to load the garage. I was so relieved to have so many hands.

Micah took control and organized the volunteers to put our plan in place.

"All the books will go on these shelves. Put shirts on this back wall, make sure to load them smallest to largest here. Sizes are on the boxes."

"What about the packing supplies?" Tessa asked.

"Let's do those last."

Within a few hours, my house was empty of boxes and products, while the garage was once again full. It was much more organized and neater than before.

"This is great. Thanks, everyone, for the help." I'd had to go in for a client meeting and had come out as the last of the boxes were being unloaded.

They got all the boxes broken down and put outside the garage door. We'd get them out to the curb in a few days when they did the recycle pickup.

Our helpers said their goodbyes while the three of us got back to our usual workday. I had three more appointments today before I could wrap up and do the rest of the cleanup in the living room.

Thankfully, there were no dramatic readings or snippy clients. Everyone left happy with closure and, hopefully, good feelings. Those were the types I loved. They made my job enjoyable.

While Janie was still here to watch Oakley, I pushed all my furniture back into place and pulled out the vacuum cleaner.

"It looks much better," Janie said, coming into the room holding Oakley.

"Yes, I'm so relieved to have that project done." I took the baby from her.

"She's freshly changed and probably will be ready for a bottle soon." Janie said. "She had a good day."

"Thanks so much."

Oakley and I walked her out. We watched as she drove off.

"Just you and me now, little girl. Maybe we should get Chewy and go for a quick walk before your bottle."

She giggled, so I took that as a yes. We got the stroller and Chewy, then did a nice lap around the block. The weather was gorgeous after the week of rain we'd had.

As I passed some of the neighbors, I greeted them. When I got close to Mrs. Washington's, I saw she was sitting on her porch. I called out to her and asked about her day.

"I'm waiting on my dog walker to come take these little guys for me." She said.

"Fabio? Nice guy."

"Oh? You know him?"

"Yeah, he'll be opening for us on our next tour."

"That's so nice, dear. He's done some magic tricks for me. He's nice to keep an old lady entertained." She smiled. "Well, I'll let y'all get back to your walk. Take care."

"Take care."

We made our way back around to our house. Once back inside, I fixed Oakley's bottle, then after she'd eaten, she went on the floor to play while I started my afternoon chores.

Tons of little laundry, dishes which were mostly bottles, and emptying the diaper pail were now my new daily tasks. I loved it. I was the girl who thought she'd never have kids.

I was finally putting my feet up when there was a knock at the door. Chewy started barking and spinning.

"Now what?" I sighed, but I didn't move right away. Instead, I grabbed my phone to check the front door camera. It was Matt, Brittney's boyfriend.

"What could he want?" I asked Chewy, who came over to see why I wasn't going to the door. He looked over his shoulder at the door. "You're right. Let's go see."

I opened the door. "Hi, Matt."

"Hi, Joanna. I'm sorry to drop in on y'all."

"That's okay. What's up?"

"I'm the one watching you today, ya know, Hank's order."

"Oh, thanks. I don't always know who's watching me or if that's even still happening."

"Yeah, still happening." He shoved his hands into his pockets. "While I was sitting here, I got to thinking about the Playhouse Killer. Thought I'd ask if y'all had any more information about the killings? Like, did any of the victims ID the guy yet?"

"Um, no, unfortunately, they didn't see him."

"How many have you talked to?" He asked.

I had to think for a moment. "Five, including Brittney."

"Oh, wow, and not one could give a description?"

"I got a vague description from one of the victims. Thinning hair, not too tall, middle-aged."

His face paled. "That could be anyone, even me."

"Yeah, like I said, it's vague, so not much to go on. I, for one, know at least eight men right now that this could be."

He rubbed his chin as he thought. He sighed and looked over his shoulder.

"Is there anything else, Matt?" I asked with a smile.

"No, no. Thanks for this. I'll get back to my watch. Stay safe." He looked me up and down, then turned and walked away.

That was odd as heck. I'd had two encounters with this guy, and both times he'd focused on the identification of the killer and what the victims knew about it. Was he worried because he was the killer?

No, he couldn't be. He was one of Hank's guys. I was sure some of them may have killed people as part of their "business," but I couldn't see Hank putting up with this type of behavior if he knew, especially when one of the victims was his own daughter.

Then I realized I was letting a good opportunity pass me by. I ran to the office window so I could peek out. He was nowhere in sight. Damn. I wanted to see which way he went. All this time, and I was never sure where Hank's guys parked to watch me.

I sighed and went back to my life. Safe for the moment and under the watchful eye of an unseen protector, or so I hoped.

Chapter Thirty-Two

I was startled awake by Chewy's growling. My adrenaline went into overdrive.

"What is it, Chewy?" I whispered.

He stood stiff, and the fur on his back was standing up. He looked over his shoulder at me, then growled low in his throat at the door.

"Oh shit." I remembered to grab my phone this time. It also allowed me to check the cameras.

There wasn't anything visible, and none of the door or window alarms were triggered, but they all looked intact. I also didn't hear anything on Oakley's monitor, so I figured at the moment she was safe.

I opened my bedroom door, and Chewy bolted out.

"Chewy!" I whisper-yelled. I had no idea what he was heading into.

He ran to the front door and started barking in a voice I hadn't heard him use yet. It was a low growl mixed with a deep bark. The sound sent goosebumps rising and a fear spreading through me like I'd never felt. Clearly, something was going on out front, and despite my fear, I was so thankful for that dog.

I peeked out the front window and saw a shadow of a person run from across the front of the house to the side toward my garage area. That was how you accessed the backyard, and Oakley's bedroom was on that side.

Chewy took off running in that direction. I followed while fumbling to call 9-1-1 on my phone.

"9-1-1, what's the address of your emergency?" The calm voice of the operator said.

"5567 Tanner Lane," I said in my shaky voice.

"How can I help?"

"Someone is creeping around my house."

"Were you able to see them?" She asked.

"Not well. Just a shadow, but my dog is going crazy."

"I can hear. I will have police dispatched to your location."

She remained on the line with me, keeping me calm while we waited for the police officers to arrive. It was several minutes of Chewy running and barking at various places. He woke up Oakley, so I was juggling a crying baby and the phone while trying to remain calm and talk to the operator.

Suddenly, there was a loud sound in the front yard and a flash of light.

"Oh my gawd."

"What happened?" The operator asked.

"It sounds like there was an explosion or something." I ran to the office window, peeking through a slit in the blinds, and saw a huge bonfire in my yard. How had he gotten all of that into the front yard? I guess that explained what all the running around was. I had been too afraid to peek out the window before this. "There's a huge fire in my yard. Please, send the fire department?"

"A fire?" She asked calmly.

"Yes," I replied, not so calmly.

"I'm dispatching them to your location." She assured me. "The officers should be there shortly."

I paced around with the baby. As long as she was okay, I'd be okay. I felt a tightness in my throat. The fear and helplessness of not knowing who was doing this to me or why was the cause. Finally, Oakley calmed, and I was able to lay her back down.

"I can hear sirens," I told the operator.

"Good. Stay on the line until they arrive and we confirm you're safe."

"Okay."

It felt like an eternity before any emergency vehicles arrived, the police and fire arriving within seconds of each other. The firefighters immediately rushed into action, getting the blaze under control.

Neighbors started to emerge from their houses. I was sure that soon they'd be holding a meeting to kick me out of our quiet little neighborhood, or if I were lucky, they enjoyed the bit of entertainment I brought. Who knows?

"Both the police and fire department are here. Thank y'all for staying with me."

"You're welcome, and be safe."

We disconnected as the officers knocked on my door. I opened it to see a familiar face.

"Officer Smith, good to see you."

"Are you sure? Under the circumstances, I wouldn't think so." She had no sense of humor, just as I remembered her. "Where did you see the guy?"

I walked her through the events that led up to their arrival, from waking up to Chewy growling to seeing the shadowy figure and how the dog kept running back and forth.

"I guess he piled up the scraps from my garage project into the front yard."

She looked over her shoulder at the heap of smoldering wood and debris. It was hard for me to tell exactly what was in the pile, but some were clearly leftover wood from the shelves and maybe the cardboard boxes we'd just stacked up. It also looked, and smelled, like he might have thrown in my trash as well. The garbage can was kept next to the garage, so easily accessible.

The fire chief came over to speak with Officer Smith. He was giving her his initial report of the fire while I stood by, barely holding onto my emotions.

I fluctuated between wanting to scream, cry, or hysterically laugh. That kind of crazy laugh that makes no sense at the time, and you stare, wondering what's wrong with that person.

What was wrong with me was I was being terrorized by a crazy person. They were winning if their goal was to scare me.

I tried to focus on what people were saying around me, but I couldn't. There was too much movement, too many voices, and I could still hear Chewy in the house. I knew it was likely because there was so much going on in the yard.

"Excuse me, Officer Smith?"

"Yes?"

"Do y'all mind if I bring my dog out? On a leash, of course, but he's in there going crazy. I'm sure he's worried about me."

"Sure, as long as he's on a leash and under control."

I stepped in and was immediately greeted by a worried and overwhelmed sixty-pound puppy.

"It's okay, Chewy. I'm back. Let's get your leash."

I clipped it to his collar. I also grabbed the baby monitor and peeked at her to make sure she was still safe. She was completely unaware of what was happening. I did a quick check of the window in her room, and then Chewy and I went back out front.

When I stepped outside, there were more people. Clint and Terry had joined the team, plus Hank and Al.

"Joanna." Clint closed the distance between us in less than a heartbeat. "Are you okay?"

"Yes, yes. I'm fine."

"Ms. Joanna, I'm so sorry," Hank said, stepping forward.

"Thanks."

"I had a man out here, but he seems to have disappeared. I'm looking for him now." Hank said, looking at Al.

Al nodded while holding a phone to his ear. He was listening to someone on the other end, but he never spoke himself. A grunt here or there, but no words. Would I ever hear him speak?

"You aren't staying here tonight," Clint said.

"It's nearly four in the morning. Hardly night."

"True, but I'm staying with you, and then we need to figure out what to do with you tonight."

"I'll be fine. Chewy helped alert me. Just like he's supposed to." I looked down at my dog, and he looked at me. I swear he looked proud of himself, as if he knew he'd done good. "Yes, you're a good boy."

He wagged his tail at me.

At that moment, a black SUV rolled up.

"It's Matt," Hank said. He and Al stepped over to the vehicle.

I couldn't hear what was said, but the angry gestures gave me an idea of how the conversation was going. This was the second time someone was supposed to be watching me and didn't see anything. Chewy was better security than they had proven to be thus far.

I leaned over and patted his head.

It was nearly daybreak by the time the last emergency vehicle left.

I decided that I'd stay at Audrey's for a few days. Once it was an appropriate time of the morning, I'd call her to ask.

Chapter Thirty-Three

~Joanna~

I stared at the ceiling in Audrey's guest bedroom, wondering how I got here and if I would need to move. I was seriously starting to consider it. Perhaps I should consider renting an office space for readings as well. Separate work and home.

It was getting complicated having them in the same space, and it allowed the public to know where I lived. It had been a few days staying here, and it proved that I could commute to work. It may no longer make sense to work from home. I'd have to think about it further and discuss it with my staff.

Chewy jumped on the bed with me. "Good morning, Chewy." I scratched behind his ears as he tried to lick my face. "Are you ready to go out?"

He yipped and ran to the door. I peeked at Oakley, still sleeping. I grabbed the baby monitor and headed out the bedroom door with Chewy.

Audrey and Stan were in the kitchen. I hated to interrupt their alone time, but Chewy really needed to go out.

"Mornin', Jo." Stan said. "Good morning, Chewy."

Chewy replied with a tail wag but continued his trek to the back door.

"Good morning. Someone needs to go." I gestured and stepped out the door with the dog.

He ran right out while I stood on the patio and waited for him. It was already warm and humid. Not my favorite, but it beat all the rain we'd been having.

"Hey, brought you coffee," Audrey said, stepping outside with me.

"Thanks."

"How're you doing?"

"I'm okay. I keep racking my brain trying to figure out who would do this to me."

"It's scary. That could have been so much worse."

"I know." I didn't even want to think about all the different scenarios.

"So, what are you going to do?"

"I guess move and maybe rent an office space for the business. Separate the two."

"That's a big step, sis," she said.

I nodded and took a long sip of coffee. Stan came out to say goodbye to Audrey before he left for work.

Chewy was done and came running back. Time for his breakfast, and I needed to get Oakley up, so I headed inside to get on with my morning. I had clients today and needed to get home before they arrived.

While I fed Oakley, Harris and Dylan woke up. They were happy to see Chewy was still here.

"Mama, we should get a dog. They're the best." Harris said as he threw a ball, and Chewy chased after it.

"Dog, mommy. Peas?" Dylan asked.

"Maybe we can talk daddy into it," she said.

"Yeah, and I will take care of it and feed it and play with it," Harris said as he ran around with my dog.

Oakley was watching and not eating well. I didn't blame her. It looked fun, but we had to get a move on, so I had to get her fed and us out the door soon.

An hour later, we pulled up at home, only to find several people in my yard. It was Al, Eddie, Darius, and Matt. They were cleaning up my yard and putting down fresh sod.

"Hey, Ms. Joanna," Eddie called out when I stepped out of the car.

"Hey, guys. What's going on?"

"Hank wanted to make up for not having someone here to stop this the other night," Darius said with a sideways glance at Matt.

"Yeah, I'm sorry, Joanna. That was my fault. I got hungry and needed to use the head, so I thought a quick trip to the gas station would be okay. I didn't know." Matt said, hanging his head.

"I understand. Everyone needs to have a break at work."

I gathered the dog and baby, then went into the house. I was relieved that my yard wouldn't show evidence from the fire. That wouldn't have been the impression I wanted to give my clients.

Janie showed up and took Oakley to her room for the day. Micah showed up soon after.

"Hey, boss," he said. "The yard looks better. Who'd you hire?"

I leaned to peek out the window. I hadn't realized that Hank's crew had left already.

"Hank sent guys."

"Guilt?"

"Yeah, at least that's what Darius said."

"They should feel guilty. If he's going to commit guys to protect you, they should be protecting you."

I couldn't argue that. He had made a commitment to have his team watch me, yet they hadn't stopped a thing. How was he so successful in his business deals if he couldn't even keep one woman safe?

"So, I was also thinking that we should consider renting an office space. Moving the business out of my house."

"That's probably a good idea, boss."

"Yeah, I'm also considering moving. Completely starting over and becoming more anonymous about my private life."

"I hate to admit that you might be right."

"I'll just see how things go." I looked around my office. "I love this house, this neighborhood. It will be a big change."

"Maybe wait until after the tour to decide anything."

"Yeah, good point. We are so close to it. I wouldn't want to be in the middle of all that change while out on the road."

"A lot to think about."

Now that I'd talked to both Audrey and Micah about my thoughts, it made it more real and that much scarier. Change was scary, but what had been happening to me had been far worse.

Micah was right, though. I didn't have to decide anything now. It could wait for another time and another day. At least for now, I had a safe place to stay.

Chapter Thirty-Four

It had been a week since I last saw Clint, not since the night of the fire almost a week ago. We'd only texted a bit here and there, so when he called, I was surprised.

"Hi, Jo."

"Hey, Clint. How's it going?"

"Good. Busy with work, but good. How are you?"

"Same. Work and baby."

"Are you still staying with Audrey, or are you back home?"

"I decided we'd try staying home tonight. I love being at my sister's and am thankful to have the option, but it's not home."

Things had been quiet with the Playhouse Killer, and there had been no other threats against me. No one following me, no one hunting me down at Audrey's. It might be a false sense of security.

"I understand that. Please be safe."

I looked over at my snoring puppy and knew that he would protect us. He had already done that by alerting me to the fire. There was also an incident a week before when he had stood stiff with the fur on his back raised. However, nothing had come from that. I'd checked the security cameras and hadn't seen anything. I still wondered what had triggered him. No matter what it was, I was just so glad I'd made the decision to get him.

"I should be safe. I've got Chewy to protect me."

"So, he's been good?"

"Definitely. I made the right decision." I said, reaching over to pet his head. He looked up at me with his classic Chewy grin and then went back to snoozing.

"Well, good. I'm glad you got a dog."

"Me too, but that's not why you called?" I asked.

"Oh, right. I wanted to see if you were free tomorrow?"

"Why, Detective, are you asking me out again?" I had wondered if we might go out again, but I'd been so busy that I hadn't reached out to him either.

He chuckled. "Why, yes, ma'am, I am."

"Good. Let me see if I can get a sitter."

"Great. Just let me know."

We spoke briefly about nothing before disconnecting.

I had no problem finding someone to watch Oakley. Tessa volunteered quickly, not giving Micah or Janie a chance to answer. Her mom, Ms. Ruby, said she'd come with her.

I loved Ms. Ruby. She was full of spunk and energy.

"Give me that sweet baby, girl!" Ms. Ruby said, stepping into the house.

I smiled and handed her over happily.

"Oh, she's getting so big. Aren't you, sweetie?" Ms. Ruby cooed to the baby.

Oakley stared at her for a moment and then giggled her sweet baby laugh before grabbing her face and pulling on Ruby's hair.

"Aw." Ms. Ruby said with no concern for her hair or face. Chewy wagged his tail and bounced around at our feet. "Oh, and look at you. Chewy, right?"

"Yep. He's eaten, and except for needing to go out a few times, he should be easy." I said. "Tessa, you should know where everything is, right?"

"Yep, sure do." Tessa smiled. "I haven't gotten to watch her yet, though, and I can't wait." She reached over and tickled the baby's foot. Oakley turned her blue eyes to Tessa, flashing her a grin and reached out for her. She loved her Auntie Tessa.

"Well, I shouldn't be out too late."

"No worries, Jo. We'll be fine." Ms. Ruby said.

"Yes, have fun, and don't worry," Tessa said as she opened the door and gestured for me to leave.

"Fine. I got it. I'm going." I kissed the baby's head, scratched the dog behind the ears before heading out.

Clint was waiting in the driveway for me. He stepped out of his truck when I came out.

"Hey." He opened the passenger door for me.

"Hey yourself." I stepped up into the cab. "Thanks."

He jogged back around to his side. "All set."

"Yep."

We were heading to Flippers to play a few games of pinball and other video games. Flippers was an adult arcade, but their specialty was pinball games. I'd never been, but it sounded fun.

When we arrived, the place was packed, but I noticed a familiar car in the lot.

"I think that's Micah and Josh's car," I said.

"Oh. Do you want to go somewhere else?"

"No, no. It's fine." They were both some of my favorite people.

We parked and headed in. Stepping inside, there was 80s music blasting over the hums, bonks, and whistles of various video games, low lighting, and lots of flashing disco-style lights. This had a fun vibe about it. I could really use that after the last few weeks of stress.

"Wow. I feel almost like I'm thirteen back at the roller rink on a Friday night." I said.

"Yeah, me too."

"I wouldn't take you for the roller-skating type."

"Ha, yeah, not so good at it, but that's where the girls were." He said with a wink.

"Oh, of course. You, ladies' man."

We walked to the counter to buy "token cards." Rather than carry a pocket full of coins around, you scan it and it charges against the balance. We each got a card.

"Where do you want to start?" He asked.

"I don't know." I looked around.

The bar was located in the middle with wall-to-wall video games and pinball machines around it. I saw games I played as a kid but hadn't thought about in years.

"Hey, Boss." The familiar voice said from behind me.

"Hey, Micah. Josh." I reached up and hugged Micah and then Josh.

"Hey, Clint. Did you catch the game last night?" Josh asked. They had bonded over sports and cleaning my house after my first break-in.

"I did. Can't believe that Jaxson pulled off that double."

They started chatting while Micah and I stood watching. Neither of us followed sports much. All I knew was it was baseball season.

"I don't want you to be caught off guard, but Fabio is here too," Micah said quietly to me.

"Oh? What are the odds?" I started looking around again. There were too many people for me to pick him out.

"He actually came with us." Micah shrugged. "I didn't know you were coming here. You didn't say this is where y'all were coming, or I would've suggested going elsewhere."

"No, it's fine. I swear I'm just overreacting, right?" I gave him a weak smile.

"Oh, Joanna, I'm sorry. Micah invited me." Fabio said as he walked up to us.

"It's fine. He told me."

"I don't want to make you uncomfortable." He turned to Micah. "I'll wait for y'all by the bar."

"No, I'm sorry. Stay. It's okay." I touched his arm.

He jumped at the touch and then blushed.

"Oh, um, okay. Thanks."

Clint and Josh had stopped talking baseball long enough to listen in on this last part of the conversation, and Clint was staring at me. I took his hand and gently squeezed it.

"Do y'all want to join us for a drink before hitting the games?" Clint asked. "On me."

The group agreed. We found a spot along the bar to sit, placed our orders, and then chatted around.

"So, Fabio, I hear you're joining this group on tour," Clint said.

"Um," Fabio looked at me and nodded, "Yeah, I'm pretty excited. It's a great opportunity. I wasn't sure if I could tell people yet."

"It's fine. I was having an off day when I said that." I said to him.

"Does that mean I can tell people? My fans?" Fabio asked.

"Yeah, Micah will give y'all the official press releases." I looked over at Micah, and he nodded his reply.

"I've caught your act at Barkers before, well the whole show, not like that one night," Clint winked at me. "You're good. Great act."

"Thanks, that means a lot." Fabio grinned widely.

We moved on to talk about less exciting things while enjoying drinks. After the first round, we got a second and then parted ways. I'm sure we would run into them around the arcade, but for now, Clint and I were back to date mode.

"So, what was all that about with Fabio?" Clint asked once we were away from the others.

"Oh, you know I told you how I keep running into him." He nodded. "I snapped at him once at the grocery store. I was just having a bad day, and he really seems like a nice guy, right?"

"Yeah, you've had a lot going on. It's normal to be a little suspicious of a stranger." He looked around, and his gaze stopped. "Huh, weird."

I followed his eyes right to Fabio, who was staring at us. When our eyes locked, he smiled, nodded, before looking back at the game he was in front of.

"Not completely abnormal, but still strange, right?" I said.

"Yeah, I'll keep an eye on him." He pulled out his phone and typed in a text message. I didn't try to see who. "I asked Hank for dirt on this guy. If anyone knows about him, it's Hank."

"Okay."

"Now let's not let this ruin our evening. Let's go get our game on."

I laughed and followed him as he headed to the wall of pinball machines. Game on.

~Stalker~

She should not be going out with the Detective. What was it going to take to get her to stop seeing him? I knew the answer.

It was finally time to come out of the shadows and tell her how I felt. She clearly wasn't understanding the clues and needed to be told and shown how things could be.

I couldn't wait any longer. It was finally time to send a much more direct message. That was the only way to get through to her.

Chapter Thirty-Five

~Joanna~

I was still on cloud nine from my date with Clint. After putting aside thoughts of Fabio, we played about a dozen different games, and exactly as I remember, I suck at video games, though I haven't laughed that much in a long time.

Ms. Ruby and Tessa had fun babysitting and dog sitting. They were disappointed when I got home.

"Now, next time you need a babysitter, I hope y'all will call us." Ms. Ruby said. "She's the sweetest little thing."

"And Chewy was super sweet too," Tessa added, scratching the dog behind his ears before they left.

The next morning, I was sipping my coffee and watching the baby roll and scoot around on the floor, Chewy keeping a close eye on her as he always did. With the boxes moved, it was nice to have all the space for them to play.

I was mindlessly lost in my head, not thinking about any one thing when I heard someone clear their throat. I jumped off the couch so fast that I nearly spilled my coffee, startling both dog and baby.

"Oh, gosh, I'm so sorry. I didn't mean to scare you." It was a woman about my age, but she was a ghost.

I swear I was never going to get used to these spirits sneaking up on me. I needed to come up with a system for them to announce themselves differently.

"It's okay. You'd think I'd be used to it." I picked up Oakley to comfort her. "It's okay, baby girl. I didn't mean to scare you."

"She's cute."

"Thanks so much." I patted Oakley's back. "So what can I do for you? I normally don't see clients this early."

"I'm sorry again. I'm so very new to this, but I was told to come see you immediately."

"Who told you that?"

"Someone named Emma. She said you'd want to talk to me right away."

A chill ran the length of my body, and the hairs on my neck stood on end. "I'm afraid to ask, but why? Are you a victim of the Playhouse Killer too?"

"Yes."

"Oh, I'm so sorry to hear." I was scrambling to place her. I didn't remember her on my list. "I'm sorry, I don't remember you as one of the victims."

"No, I don't even know if the cops know about me yet."

I gasped. "When... when...?" I couldn't even finish my sentence.

"Last night."

I checked the time. Clint should be awake by now.

"Do you know where your body is?"

"Kinda."

"Kinda? Didn't you just come from it?"

"Yes, but it's weird. Right when you die, things are fuzzy and unreal. I was away from the area before I fully knew what happened. That's when I ran into Emma. She asked if I was lost, as I must have looked like it, and I told her what happened. She said I needed to come here right away."

"I wonder why she said that."

"Because I was told to give you a message from the killer."

The room spun, and the light dulled.

"A message? For me?"

"Yes. I'm not sure how I remember this because, like I said, some things about my death are blurry and hard to remember, but he said this over and over, asking me to repeat it."

My stomach churned. I knew I'd have to hear the message, but I also knew whatever it was would change the whole direction of my life.

"I hate to ask." I took a deep breath. "What's the message?"

"He said if you don't stop seeing the detective, he will kill someone close to you. He wants you for himself, and he just needs some time before he can tell you in person. He's almost ready to reveal himself to you. Be patient."

I ran for the bathroom. Chewy followed close on my heels. I was glad for the company but could have handled this by myself. As it was, I had to bring the baby with me too. One of those ugly parts of motherhood, I supposed. Thankfully, the new spirit hadn't followed me. I had enough of an audience.

After my stomach was done with me, I went back to the living room with the baby and dog in tow.

"Sorry about that. I'm okay now." I took a breath. "Was there anything else?"

"No, that was really it. He seems obsessed with you. He kept ranting on and on about you. It was so obsessive, that's why I think I can remember it."

"So it seems. Too much." Fabio was as well.

"I know you probably want to know what he looks like and stuff, but he grabbed me when I was walking to my car after work. It was dark, and he stuck me with some kind of needle. I got dizzy, and then I woke up here and there until we were in the empty warehouse. That's when he tortured me."

"I'm so sorry. That had to have been so scary."

She nodded. "It was."

We were both quiet for a moment. So many thoughts were running through my head that I couldn't even form one clear thought to verbalize.

"Well, I better go. Not that I have anywhere to go, but ya know, go figure out this how to be dead thing."

"I'll call the police for you. I'm sure someone is missing you already."

"Yes, my family. I don't want to be around when they're told. Good luck, Joanna. I hope he's caught before he gets to you."

Another shiver ran through me. Now I had a dilemma. Do I call Clint? The message was to not see Clint any longer. What if I call Terry instead, or maybe Hank to have him report it for me? Should I call 9-1-1 to report it?

I decided to call Clint after all. He knew me and would know what to do. It wasn't like the killer could see my phone call.

"Hello?" Clint said, answering my call.

"Hey, sorry to bother you so early."

"No problem. What's up? Is something wrong?"

"Yes!" I realized at that moment that I hadn't asked her name. I was so shocked by her message that it slipped my mind completely. "I was just visited by a new ghost. She says she was killed last night by the Playhouse Killer."

He sighed heavily and mumbled something I couldn't quite hear. "Is she sure? What's her name? Do you know where her body is?"

"She's sure. No, I forgot to ask her name, and she doesn't know where the body is exactly. Just an empty warehouse."

"How did you not get her name? That's the most important question."

"I know, I know, but I was too busy processing the message the killer sent with her."

"What? Are you serious?"

"Yeah, so you'll have to forgive me a bit for missing some details." Important details, but still, fear had taken over my body and mind at that moment.

"What was the message?"

"He said that I need to stop seeing you, or else he would kill someone close to me."

He cursed and possibly punched something on the other end of the phone. "Okay, Joanna, we are going to need to move you. Maybe put you into a type of witness protection lockdown."

"I can't do that. I have clients, and he didn't say he would hurt me, but someone I love. So if we are going to hide anyone away, it needs to be my family and friends."

"Jo, that's crazy. This guy is a nut job. I have to make sure you are safe."

I looked down at the smiling face of my sixty-pound watchdog. I had a feeling he wouldn't let anyone get to me. I also knew I had Hank's guys watching me. Eddie and Al saved me the night of the break-in, so I knew they'd come to get me, but what if Matt was on watch?

Plus, I was tired of running. It wasn't logical or smart, but I knew that I had to be brave and stand my ground. If I go into hiding, wouldn't that upset this guy even more? He might kill more people. No, I had to stay and hope that if he did come for me, the various security measures I had in place would be enough to get him caught. I would just have to be extra vigilant.

"I honestly think I'm safe, or safe enough, but you need to find this girl's body." I gave a description of her. The same as all the other girls, including myself. As I was describing the nameless victim, I realized I needed to stay elsewhere. "You know what, maybe I'll go stay with my sister for a few days."

"Good idea." I could hear him fumbling with things in the background and then the unmistakable sound of keys. "Okay, I'll call you later. I'm heading to find her. Thanks for the tip."

"Anytime."

"And Jo, please stay safe for Oakley, for your family, and... for me." Did his voice choke a little?

"I will. You too."

It was late afternoon before I finally got an update on the nameless ghost. Her name was Taylor Darby. She had been a bartender at Flippers.

"Clint, we were at Flippers last night." I fought tears. "This is my fault."

"No, it's not. You didn't make this guy evil. He is like that on his own."

Logically I knew that was true, but I had a sick, sick feeling, and all signs pointed to one person: Fabio.

"Have you checked out Fabio's alibi after we left last night?"

"Already working on it," he said.

Chapter Thirty-Six

~Clint~

I paced back and forth as I waited for Fabio to arrive. I'd called him and let him know we had some questions about a case. There was no evidence or probable cause to arrest him, but we were within our rights to ask him questions. He could choose to answer or not. I had to hope he would work with us, though, as I needed answers, and he might have them. People's lives were on the line here.

My desk phone rang.

"Hartley," I said, answering it.

"Your guy is here." The officer at the front desk said.

"I'll be right there."

I stuck my head next door in Terry's office.

"Fabio's here. You want to join me for this?"

"Oh, yeah. Which room? I can meet you there."

"Two," I said.

He nodded and grabbed a notebook and pen from his desk while I turned toward the lobby. As I made my way through the crowded station, my adrenaline surged. This was the first time we'd had anything close to a suspect in this case. I knew better than to think it was this easy, but still, I had hope.

I stepped through the door that separated the lobby from the back offices. I took a deep breath and said a little prayer that I would be making an arrest at the end of this interview.

The lobby was bustling, and it took a moment to locate Fabio among the crowd. He blended in well. I waved to get his attention, but he seemed lost in thought. I crossed the room.

"Fabio." I tapped him on the shoulder.

"Oh, sorry, Detective. I didn't see you." He yawned. "I didn't sleep much last night."

My heart pumped hard at his words. What had he been doing? Flippers wasn't open all night, so he hadn't been there.

"This shouldn't take long." I gestured for him to follow me.

He followed me as we made our way to room two.

"Here we are," I said.

Fabio saw Terry in the room and hesitated to walk in. "I'm sorry, am I under arrest for something? I thought y'all just wanted to talk."

"We do. I asked Detective Walden as extra ears and to take notes."

Fabio nodded and slowly stepped in.

"Have a seat anywhere," Terry said.

Fabio looked around and took a seat closest to the door. Honestly, I didn't blame him, but even if he tried to run, he wouldn't get far. These interview rooms are placed as far from the exits as possible for a reason.

Terry and I sat across from Fabio. Terry readied his pen.

"So, Fabio, we want to ask a few questions about your whereabouts from last night and if you saw anything suspicious. You are not under arrest. You're not a suspect. We just need information."

"Okay." He said slowly, eyeing both of us. "As y'all know, I was at Flippers with you, Joanna, Micah, and Josh."

"Yes. And what time did you leave?"

"We left around eleven and went over to Pie in the Sky for a late-night snack." He smiled. "Have y'all had their banana cream? It's heaven."

"And you were with Micah and Josh the entire time from Flippers to Pie in the Sky?"

"Yes."

"What time did you leave there?" I asked.

He scratched his face as he thought. "I think it was close to one."

"You left with both of them again?"

"Yeah, they drove, so I was kinda at their mercy."

"Okay. So did they take you home at this point?"

"Nah, I had a buddy who was doing a late gig at Barkers, so we went over there."

"How late were you at Barkers?"

"It was close to three when we left. The guys dropped me at my place after that."

"Okay, okay. Good."

I looked over at Terry's notes. He was writing the high points. I wasn't sure where to go from here. I knew Flippers closed at midnight, and from talking to the manager, Taylor had left when they closed. If Fabio was with Micah and Josh, there was no way he could be the killer.

"Terry, do you have any questions?"

Terry looked up, stared for a moment before speaking. "Did you see anyone suspicious hanging around at Flippers before you left? Anyone that seemed out of place?"

"Nah, I wouldn't even know what to look for." He sat forward. "Did something happen at Flippers last night? Y'all thought I might have done it, didn't you?"

I couldn't say much, but I had to say something. "Yes, something happened. We are asking people we know were there last night to see if they know anything. The times you gave wouldn't have put you there near the time of the crime, but we had to ask in case you had some information."

That should cover my ass, and I did have every intention of asking employees and calling in Micah and Josh too.

"Look, man, I swear, I was with Micah and Josh the entire time. I didn't see anything. I didn't do nothing."

I believed him, but damn it, I wanted so badly to find this guy.

"Got it. You're fine. We appreciate you coming in. It helps us out." I stood up. "I'll walk you out."

He stood, reached over to shake Terry's hand, and then followed me out. I was disappointed that this case wasn't over. At this rate, we may never find this guy.

When we got to the lobby, I reassured him once again that he was not a suspect, we were only looking for information.

"If I think of anything else that might be helpful, I'll let y'all know." He said before leaving.

I stood watching the station door, frustrated that this hadn't been fruitful. I wanted to solve this and protect the women of Creekview.

As I turned to head back to my office, Terry came into the lobby.

"It's Joanna."

"Shit."

Chapter Thirty-Seven

I had just put the baby down for her mid-morning nap when I heard some noise from the garage. I peeked out the window. It was Donovan taking tools out of his van. What was he doing? He'd finished the garage work already, and I didn't have him working on anything else.

I went out to speak to him, but when I got close, his expression sent a chill through me. It was not his usual carefree, happy-go-lucky self. He had a darkness in his eyes. In all this time working with him, I had not seen that evil or felt this fear.

I tried to shake it off and put on my best Joanna the Medium stage smile. "Hey, Donovan, I wasn't expecting you today."

"I need to unload some of these tools. I need the space."

"Oh, um, you want to leave them here? I don't think—"

"Yes, I'm leaving them here. You won't mind because you won't live here much longer." His face went stone-cold.

I tried to reply calmly. "You're silly, Donovan. I'm not moving."

He closed the distance between us in less than a heartbeat. "No, Jo, you don't understand. You're coming with me, and I never plan to let you go."

He grabbed me, throwing me into the back of his van. He hopped in too, never taking his hands off of me, and before I could fully process what was happening, he had me tied up and gagged. Clearly, he was a professional at this, and that's when I realized he was my stalker. He was the Playhouse Killer.

The next thought was about Oakley. Nobody would know she was alone unless Hank's guys happened to see. But Donovan had been smart. He pulled all the way up my driveway, and it wasn't easy to see this side of the house from the road. I wasn't sure where Hank's guys sat when they were watching me, but I sure hoped they saw.

I could hear Chewy barking and carrying on in the house. He knew, and if he could get to me, he would. I looked at Donovan as he finished tying me. I hoped he didn't go in after the dog or the baby.

"Don't worry, my love." He caressed my face. "My mother will come over later to get the baby." He said before climbing into the driver's seat. "She's always wanted a little girl."

Panic shot through me at the thought. My sweet daughter would be in the hands of the person who raised this monster. Even her own bio mother wasn't as scary as the thought of these two. I eyed the door. I thought I might be able to get it open even with my hands tied. I wiggled to try to reach the latch or free my hands.

"Now, don't try anything stupid, or things will get really ugly, really fast." He snarled.

I nodded to him and settled down, but my mind raced. I had to come up with a plan before we got too far. He put the van in motion, and my heart raced. I needed to do something, get the attention of Hank's guys, figure out how to call Clint. I couldn't let this happen, not again, but I couldn't see as there weren't windows in the back of the van.

Looking around the van, I couldn't find anything I could easily use as a weapon or to free myself. I guess he'd made sure to take out anything useful before putting me in it. My only option was to try to get the door open, but I didn't think I could jump from a moving vehicle, especially not with my hands and feet tied up. As he drove, any hope sank.

The only silver lining I could come up with was that he hadn't drugged me like the other victims, so maybe he had different plans for me than he had with them. Any hope was better than none.

We drove in silence for a long time. I tried to stretch to see out the front windshield. It appeared we were heading to Buckston. Apparently, that's where all the criminals ran.

It made sense because the side that bordered Creekview used to be industrial but had been widely abandoned over the past five or six years. It left a lot of empty buildings and nobody keeping an eye on them.

I knew from Clint and the victims that he'd previously used a few places in Creekview but had never gone into Buckston. This was a new one.

I wished I weren't gagged. If I could talk to him, I might be able to find out what he was thinking and talk him out of whatever he had planned. Micah had told me several times how persuasive I was with people, saying I had a charm. If I could use it, maybe I could get out of this with my life and back to my baby and dog.

I wiggled around and tried to free my hands. What was the trick to it again? I turned them this way and that, trying anything to get them loose. Nothing worked.

Finally, we stopped. I tried to see where we were, but his body blocked my view as he climbed into the back with me.

"Are you ready to start your new life with me, my darlin'?" He caressed my cheek with the back of his hand. I tried to move away, but when I did, his face went red, and he pushed me onto my back and climbed on top of me. "I could make you so happy if you'd let me."

I tried to speak, but with the gag still in my mouth, I could only mumble.

"I will take that off later, but first, I have to know you won't run away from me."

I nodded my head, even though I knew if given a chance, I was making a run for it. He stroked my hair and smelled my neck. It was sickening, causing my stomach to lurch.

"Okay, you stay here. I'm going to check that I can get you out without being seen." He laughed. Was it supposed to be a joke? Where were we?

He jumped up and climbed back through the front of the van. I thought maybe I could break out while he was gone, but then I heard him hit the locks.

"NO!"

Okay, Joanna, you can still do this for Oakley, I thought.

I squirmed and twisted until I was in a seated position. This was a little better. I looked around at this level to see if there was anything I could leverage to make my escape. I did the butt hop thing to move myself around. I was close to the side door when the back doors opened.

"What are you doing?" He snapped. "I told you no funny business or things would get bad."

I shook my head and tried to plead with him. Tears formed in my eyes, though they were more from frustration than fear. I needed to get back to Oakley. I had to protect her.

"Who am I kidding? I could never hurt you." His tone softened. He climbed into the back of the van and pulled me roughly.

I yelped from the pain. So much for not hurting me.

When he got me out of the van, it took my eyes a moment to adjust to the brightness. I was expecting to see nothing but abandoned metal warehouses and cracked concrete parking lots, but instead, it was tall pine and oak trees and a single mobile home in a small clearing. There were other smaller buildings that might be storage sheds or maybe a barn.

So who had he been worried would see us out here? Were there other houses nearby? That thought gave me hope if I were able to get free of him.

I tried to take in my surroundings as fast as I could. I might be able to break from him, and the thick trails leading away from here looked promising. He might be strong, but he was older and slightly overweight. Perhaps I could outrun him.

"I can see that look in your eyes. Don't even think about it. One call, and that baby of yours is gone."

I gasped as a helpless feeling washed over me. I had to play along and hope for the best. The best was that someone had gotten to her before his evil mother did.

"Let's go." He dragged me toward the house. I nearly lost my balance but somehow managed to stay on my feet. It was important to keep as much control as I could.

We stepped up the creaking stairs, and he swung the door open. Inside was dark and dusty, a strong smell of mold filled the air, causing me to choke a bit.

He pushed me forward and onto a threadbare couch.

"There. You're now home with me, and we can start our life together." He sat next to me. "I have waited for this day for so long, and it's finally here."

His phone rang. "It's Mother. She must have gotten the baby."

"Hello?" He said into the phone. "What? She was there when I left... What about the dog?... I don't know. I don't know, Ma."

He got up and walked down the hall, so I couldn't hear the rest of the conversation, but it sounded like both Oakley and Chewy had been rescued before his mother could get there. I could only hope and pray that was the case.

I listened. It sounded like he was still on the phone. His voice was angry. Maybe I could run now. My hands and feet were tied, and the angle I'd landed when he pushed me down meant I had to roll off the couch. I inched my way along the floor until I got close to the door. From here, I had to throw my body left to right until I could get enough momentum to stand.

Out of breath but not out of hope, I turned so that I could reach the handle of the door with my hands behind my back. Success. I had it in my hand and was ready to turn it when Donovan came back in the room.

His face went red. "No, no, no!" He charged me.

With my back pressed against the door, I quickly twisted the door handle, and when it opened, I fell out. I tried to scramble to my feet, but he jumped out and landed on me. The force of his body knocked the wind out of me. This time when the tears started, it was from the pain.

He pushed himself off of me, forcefully grabbed me, and pulled me to his eye level. I was shaking with fear.

"Don't you dare try that again! You will be so sorry. You know what I did to those other girls. I can do the same to you."

He pushed me roughly up the steps and back into the house of hell. I wasn't going to give up. I'd try over and over again because I had to get to Oakley.

Chapter Thirty-Eight

~Donovan~

I finally had her. I could hold her and touch her. There was a peaceful feeling all through my body when I looked at her. It was the first time I had ever felt this kind of calm.

Though she'd tried a few times to get away, she couldn't get far. She didn't know, but it was quite a hike from here to the nearest town. I'd chosen this place specifically for that reason. Isolated. Remote. Mine.

The others hadn't lasted long enough to see this place. They hadn't been worthy. But Joanna was different. She was special. She was meant to be here with me.

If she would just relax and open her eyes, she'd see we were meant to be. Once she realized that, she would be happier and stop trying to run from me. It was only a matter of time before she understood. Before she saw that everything I'd done was for us.

The call from Mother threw some of the plans off, but no matter. Joanna didn't deserve to have a little girl anyway. She'd been a rotten mother, choosing her career over her child, letting strangers raise her. She could barely care for herself, let alone a little person.

An evil smile spread across my face thinking about how angry Mother had been, demanding I tell her where we were. She would never find me here. Nobody knew about this place. It had been my secret for years. My sanctuary. And now, it would be ours.

I'd built most of it myself. The well. The shelving inside. Even reinforced the locks on the doors. Every board, every nail driven with purpose. With the future in mind. Our future.

Joanna made a sound, so I turned toward her. She was awake again. I hoped she had learned her lesson not to disobey me, or I would have to punish her again. I didn't want to hurt her, but she needed to understand the rules.

"Will you obey me from now on?"

She nodded her head.

"Do you want some water?"

She nodded her head again.

I went to the kitchen and filled a glass with water from the tap. It wasn't the prettiest water, but it was clean. I'd dug the well and connected it all myself. Another thing I could provide for her. Another way I could take care of her, better than that detective ever could.

I slipped the gag from her mouth. She coughed a few times, and a tear ran down her face. I wiped the tear with my thumb. She looked so beautiful, even like this. Especially like this. Finally mine.

"Here. Take a sip." I held the glass to her mouth. She took a gulp, choking and spitting water all over. I backhanded her. "You bitch."

"Ow, I didn't do it on purpose. The water is hot." She spat out. "Taste it yourself."

I smelled it and took a sip. The hot, bitter taste caused me to spit it out. Damn. The well water must have been sitting in the pipes too long. I'd need to fix that.

"I'll go get us some bottled water. We'll need groceries too." I studied her for a moment, making sure the ropes were secure. "Now, don't you go anywhere while I'm gone."

I laughed at my joke. She was tied to the couch, so she couldn't go anywhere if she wanted to.

But as I looked at her one more time before leaving, I felt that peace again. That rightness. She belonged here. With me. Soon she would see it too.

I grabbed my keys and left, making sure to lock the door behind me. I wouldn't be gone long. Just long enough to get what we needed to start our new life together.

Chapter Thirty-Nine

I tried in vain to free myself while he was gone, but no luck. He had me tied much tighter this time. I cried and yelled until I heard the van returning. I cursed in my head. What fresh hell was he bringing back?

"Honey, I'm home." He laughed as he stepped inside. He was loaded down with grocery bags. "I got food."

He went to the kitchen area and started unpacking groceries. After the food was put away, he walked toward me with a bag.

"I got you a present." He pulled out a long maroon dress with a large floral print on it. There was no shape to it, almost like a sack.

He untied me just enough that he could remove my clothing and slip the dress over my head. After he had me dressed, he pulled out a brush and started roughly brushing my hair. I yelped a few times, which made him yank harder, so I tried not to make a sound. Once he was satisfied with that, he braided my hair down my back.

"Let me see you." He spun me around, not an easy task when I was still half tied to the couch. "Perfect."

I had a sick realization that he had dressed me like his mother, though I'd only met her the one time. What kind of sick relationship did these two have?

"What is your plan with me?" I asked.

"To make you my wife, of course."

I shuddered at his words. He was delusional.

"Your wife? Donovan, I don't think—"

"After all I have done for you, I deserve this. I deserve you." He said, right against my cheek. He snuggled his head into my neck. "You will learn to love me as much as I love you."

I fought the urge to gag. He, once again, tied me to the couch and then went outside without a word. I had no idea where he was going or how long he'd be gone, but regardless, I was going to try to untie myself any chance I could.

It was roughly an hour, though I wasn't completely sure as there wasn't a clock, before he returned. I was exhausted from fighting the ropes and laying limp on the couch when he came in.

"Are you ready to behave now?" He said, coming to me.

I nodded my head, though I knew it was a lie. I would never stop fighting to be free. I had too much to live for to give up.

He removed the gag and untied my hands and feet. As soon as I felt my limbs were free, I kicked him as hard as I could and tried to run. I made it as far as the first step before he was on me again. Why couldn't I get past the top of the steps?

He pulled me back in and threw me to the ground, jumping on me and pinning me down.

"Why do you keep trying to run? That is stupid, so very stupid. There is nothing for you back there. Your baby is gone. That detective is trash. I deserve you. You must be here with me." He shook me as he yelled at me. "He can't protect you the way I can. He has let you get kidnapped twice already. That's not love, Joanna."

I whimpered and strained to get free of his grasp. This wasn't right. This couldn't be the same sweet man who had been so helpful after the storm, who had offered to fix my door and had done all that great work in my garage.

"I'm sorry. I'm sorry. I promise I'll be good. I'll stop trying to run." Tears stung my eyes, and soon I was hyperventilating.

"Oh, my love, I'm sorry. I didn't mean to scare you." He pulled me up and into his lap, cradling me and rocking me. "Don't cry. I'll protect you and love you."

He rocked me for several heartbreaking moments while I cried for myself, my daughter, my family, for all I had to lose if I didn't get free of him. I pictured Oakley's little face and her sweet baby laugh. How I hoped to hear it again soon. I hoped she was safe with people that loved her and not with his awful mother. I hadn't heard any more about whether she had gotten my baby. I had to hope she hadn't.

Finally, I had cried all I could, so I laid stiff in his arms. I had no choice as he was still holding me.

"Do you feel better?" He asked after several minutes of silence.

Not trusting myself to speak, I simply nodded my head in reply.

"Good," he said. "Now, why don't we try this again. I'll let you go, but you have to listen to me."

I nodded. This time I wouldn't run, at least not right away. Even at his age and size, he was quick. There was no point until he was away from the house or asleep. It had become clear that if he were awake, there was no way I could get away from him.

He let me go, and I sat next to him on the floor. This was better than sitting in his lap, but not much.

"Okay, now that you have decided to behave, why don't you make me some dinner? I have all the fixings for fried chicken with mashed potatoes and green beans."

"I don't know how to make fried chicken."

"Are you talking back to me?" He growled.

"No, no. I'm sorry." I could figure this out. I stood slowly and moved to the kitchen area.

"That's better." He also stood and moved to the couch. He picked up the remote for the television and turned it on.

I looked at the various supplies he'd bought. I could do this. How hard could it be?

Hours later, dinner had been cooked, eaten, and I'd cleaned up. We were now seated together on the couch. He'd pulled a blanket around us and pulled me closer to him. I wanted to throw up.

"See? Isn't this nice."

"Um, yeah." Not.

He turned toward me. "Aren't you happy here with me?"

"Oh, yes, of course." Lies. "I just miss my daughter and my dog."

"Well, darlin', we can have our own children." He leaned toward me, but thankfully there was a sound outside.

He jumped to his feet and flew to the window. "Just a couple of raccoons digging in the trash. I'll go shoo them away." He started to leave but turned back. "Don't you go anywhere, or you know what will happen."

He laughed at his joke as he stepped outside. I knew this was not the right time to try anything, so I promised myself I would stay put.

It didn't matter anyway, as he was only gone for a brief moment. It would not have been enough time to formulate a plan, even if I wanted to.

"They ran off," he said. "Now, where were we?"

"Oh, um, can we go to bed? I'm so tired." I faked a yawn.

"Sure. There will be plenty of time for baby-making later." He laughed.

He took me to the dingy, tiny bedroom. Everything looked dusty and unused, but at least the sheets seemed clean. Once we were both in the bed, he pulled me against him.

He whispered his love for me and how happy he was to be with me before dozing off. He almost immediately started snoring loudly. It was going to be a long, long night.

Chapter Forty

The next morning, after a restless night, I made us breakfast. He made sure to keep a close eye on me and had warned me again not to do anything stupid. After yesterday, I knew it was pointless, so I acted as a good pretend wife.

He also had another awful shapeless dress for me to wear, so he could live out some sick fantasy at my expense.

After breakfast, we watched television with more forced cuddles. It made my skin crawl, but thankfully, I'd been able to avoid anything more intimate, and I hoped to continue to avoid it as long as possible.

This became our routine for the next few days. Us basically playing house, and that's when I knew his nickname of Playhouse Killer fit, even if the media didn't yet know about this part of it.

As I was trying to figure out our lunch one day, I realized we would need more groceries.

"Donovan, we are running low on food. Can we run into town for groceries?"

"No, we can't, but I will run, and you will stay here. I'll have to tie you up while I'm gone."

"No, please, no. I'll stay here and won't try to run, but please don't tie me up." I begged, knowing full well if he left, I was out of here.

"I don't trust you. Have a seat on the couch."

He tied me tightly before leaving me alone. I was thankful he hadn't gagged me again. The ropes were so tight that I wasn't sure I could escape these restraints, but I was going to try, just as soon as he was gone.

I listened as the van started, then the fading sound of the engine as it traveled down the road. When I was sure he was gone, I fell apart. I cried. I screamed and yelled. I kicked and fought. I had too much to fight for to take this lying down. All the frustration of being in his husband-wife fantasy came out.

After what felt like hours, but was probably less than an hour, I gave up. I was exhausted, and every bone in my body hurt. I had nothing left to give. I lay there, weeping.

"What am I going to do?"

"You're going to keep fighting." A familiar voice said.

"Grams. Oh my gawd, how...? What are you doing here?" I never knew when I'd see her. She went long stretches between visits, but not quite as long as when I had to block my psychic powers as a young teen. I had missed her in my life all those years.

"I came to comfort you. I know I can't help much, but at least you're not completely alone."

"Thank you so much. I'm so happy to see you."

"Of course, sweetie."

"Do you happen to know anything about Oakley? And where am I?"

"Oakley is fine. She's with Audrey."

"Thank goodness. Do you know how or who found her?"

"That guy, Al, found her. He saw Donovan's van leave. At first, he didn't think anything of it, but he could hear Chewy going crazy, so he went to check."

I was so glad she knew what was going on. I didn't know how she knew, and I was too relieved to ask.

"Is Chewy okay?"

"Yes, Audrey has him too." Grams assured me.

"Oh, thank goodness." I breathed a sigh of relief. If nothing else, they were safe, and after days of wondering, I now knew. "I assume they're looking for me."

"Yes. I wish I could tell them where you are. We need a second medium in town."

I laughed a little. "There is certainly enough work for two."

"Okay, now let's try to get you out of here."

"How? You're a ghost, and I can't untie these ropes. I've tried."

"I don't know how, but we have to try. Let me see if I can talk you through this."

We spent the next hour trying to get me untied. She looked at the ropes that were behind me and offered suggestions on where to push or pull or twist. I could feel them get looser with each movement.

I peeked out the grimy windows. It was getting dark out. I sure hoped Donovan didn't get back anytime soon. He'd already been gone longer than I thought he should be. I could feel my time alone getting shorter and my window of escape getting smaller.

"Okay, you almost have it." Grams said from behind me. "Just push that a little more. There!"

I had my hands free. I quickly got the rest of my body untied. "Let's get out of here."

I sprinted toward the door, throwing it open and running for the woods. I had no idea where I was going, but I knew I had to go the opposite direction of the driveway that Donovan would be driving up at any moment.

I ran blindly, branches hitting me and tearing at my skin. The trees and brush so thick, it was hard to move, but I had freedom, so I was going as fast and as hard as I could without looking too far in front of me, just running.

Grams' spirit could barely keep up, and soon I lost her. I didn't even know when or how. Or was it possible I had simply hallucinated her? How had she found me? No time to think about that. I had to get away from Donovan.

I got to another small clearing and ducked down, thinking I was back at the mobile home. I looked around in the near darkness. No, this was a different one. There was no house in sight. It was just a random clearing.

"Okay, now which way?" I looked around, staying low since I wasn't sure where I was and not sure if Donovan would be close by. When I made my decision, I jumped to my feet and ran.

Chapter Forty-One

~ Clint ~

We finally had the Playhouse Killer. Donovan Pollack. How had I missed the signs? He had been there the whole time. Now to find Joanna.

It all started when we'd gotten a tip from Al that Joanna was missing, and he had Oakley and the dog.

He saw Donovan's van leave quickly, so he went to the house to check on her. He said he could hear the dog going crazy inside the house. After he knocked several times, he let himself in. That's when Mona Pollack showed up on the scene. He got her in the house and called us.

She claims she only knew of his plan to kidnap Joanna and for her to take the baby, but she didn't know about him killing anyone and, in fact, had been shocked at the suggestion.

"He's a fricking idiot. How could he do those things?" Mona said when we questioned her. "He's a good boy who cares for me. I'm disabled, you know."

She was being held in one room for now while we had Donovan in another. We were looking to charge her with the attempted kidnapping of Oakley and as an accomplice to kidnapping Joanna. We still hadn't determined if she had anything to do with the murders, but further investigating and questioning would tell us for sure.

Terry and I were now interviewing Donovan, trying to find where he'd taken Joanna. It had been days. Experience told me that this was more a recovery than a rescue, but I wanted to be optimistic. This was Joanna. The town couldn't lose her. Her family couldn't lose her. I couldn't lose her.

"Where did you leave her?" I snarled at him. "She better still be alive."

He simply threw his head back laughing the most sadistic laugh. The sound was like nails on a chalkboard, and I wanted so badly to punch him square in the face. I was trained better than that, but it didn't change the fact I thought it.

Terry slapped the table in front of him. "Tell us where she is!"

He'd had the same training, which is why he hit the table instead of the Playhouse Killer.

"I'll never say. I'd rather let her rot where she is than tell either of y'all." He taunted.

"What do you want with her?" I asked through gritted teeth.

"To marry her and make her love me."

I stared at him. "Marry her?"

That was not what I thought he'd say. Torture her, kill her, sure, but not marry her.

"Yes, she's meant to be with me. You... you aren't good enough for her." He growled at me.

I turned my back on him. If I didn't, I was going to lose my cool on this guy. Terry nodded for me to join him in the hallway.

"We're not getting anywhere with him," he said once we were away from Donovan. "Maybe we just go look for her."

"Where? He already said she wasn't in Creekview."

"Near Applewood since that's where we picked him up. The grocery manager said Donovan had been spending a lot of time out there. You know there are camps and small homes all around the preserve."

I rubbed my hands through my hair, feeling helpless. "Okay, yeah, that's true. I'm just letting my emotions cloud my judgment. Let's go."

We got both Donovan and Mona locked back up, then organized a search party. It was a mix of police officers and volunteers. Her dad and brother-in-law were here along with Micah, Josh, and Tessa, plus Fabio and her nanny, Janie. Hank sent over a dozen of his guys too.

Plus, others who knew her, like Greg Landon, Frank Landon, and Aaron Novak. She'd helped bring peace to their family by solving Jeremy Landon's murder, so I wasn't all that surprised to see they wanted to help.

I looked around at all the faces marked with concern for our favorite local celebrity. We had to find her. We would find her.

"We picked him up near Applewood, not far from the nature preserve. He had groceries and some camping gear, so he must have her locked up somewhere nearby. We'll start there." I said to the crowd. "We've got ATVs, dogs, and then most of us will be searching on foot."

We loaded up, and a caravan of vehicles made our way to Applewood. It was south of Creekview and bordered Buckston. There wasn't much to it. It was mostly the nature preserve and woods. The town itself was small and only had a few businesses that were kept open by campers and hikers.

We arrived and parked at the local park. It was the only lot big enough for our crowd. The local police department met us here. From here, we organized everyone into groups.

"Okay, y'all know your assignments. Check in often."

Our group was made up of Terry and me, plus her dad Charlie and Stan. They hopped in Terry's car, and we started driving the north side of town. We were going to stop at each and every house we could find.

Two hours later, we followed this barely visible dirt road to a small clearing. There was a dingy, rundown mobile home on the property. As we got close, I could see that the door was open.

"Looks abandoned," Charlie said from the back seat.

"Yeah, but we have to check," I said.

Terry parked, and only I got out. Something didn't feel right. I hovered my hand over my gun. In all my years as a cop, I had only ever drawn my gun twice before, but something about this place had me thinking today would be three.

I slowly approached the door. "Hello? Anyone home?"

I was met by silence, so I ascended the steps and peeked in the door. "Hello?"

Nothing. I started to relax and think this was just another abandoned house when I saw the rope. On the floor was a pile of ropes. I scanned the room quickly. Not much else here.

"Joanna? Jo, are you here?" I walked down the hall to the one bedroom and bathroom to search for any evidence she had been here. There were some clothes hung in the open closet and a few toiletries in the bathroom, but not much else to give any clues. But it looked like a man and woman had both been here by the clothing I saw.

I joined the others outside. They had all gotten out of the car and were standing around.

"It looks like this might have been it, but she's not here. Not sure if she escaped or someone else beat us to her... and I don't mean someone on our side."

"I'll call the other teams," Terry said, heading back to the car for his radio. We had given each team a radio to stay in touch.

We got everyone to our location and then set out in various directions to search for her. This time it was just Charlie and me. I didn't know him well, only meeting him a few times, but he seemed like a solid guy.

"It's getting dark. Do you think she'll be okay?" He asked as we made our way through a makeshift trail.

"Yes, she's strong and resourceful. I have no doubts she'll be fine."

We searched until it was too dark and then gathered back at the old mobile home. We planned to meet back first thing in the morning and to start from this point again.

As I watched the cars slowly travel down the road, I looked out into the woods.

"Stay safe, Jo," I whispered and then reluctantly got into Terry's car. I knew what I told her dad, but I was petrified for her.

Chapter Forty-Two

When I realized where he'd taken me, my fear grew. If I weren't careful and deliberate in my decisions, I could end up being lost in the nature preserve for days. There were always news stories about hikers being lost.

As night fell, I thought of all the survival shows I'd ever watched. I needed to find some kind of shelter. Not an easy feat in the darkness that was quickly taking over.

I managed to find a tree that I could lean against, and the surrounding bushes were dense, so I thought this could work for one night. I gathered up some pine needles, shaking them out in case of bugs, and piled them to lay on and pull around me to stay warm. It wasn't the most comfortable, especially with thoughts of animals and bugs, but it was one night, and I wasn't next to a killer.

Tomorrow I would use some of the other tactics I'd learned from the shows, like how to leave clues. I'd also have to get my bearings and determine which way I needed to head to get myself out of here. I honestly didn't know if those shows were realistic at all, but it couldn't hurt to try.

I lay there for a while, listening to the forest sounds, the creaking of trees, the buzz and hum of insects, and the occasional hoot or screech of owls. If I wasn't so scared, thirsty, and hungry, it might have been peaceful.

I dozed on and off all night until the sun started to peek through the thick canopy of the forest. I'd survived the night, though I was cold, hungry, and dehydrated. It was going to take some effort today to get out of here.

I stood and stretched, scanning the area to see if I could figure out which way I should head.

"The sun is east, so that's west," I said over my shoulder, "but how do I figure out north and south?"

I knew Applewood was to the south of Creekview. I figured I needed to go north. However, what if I was at the back of the preserve? Should I go east back toward Applewood itself?

Maybe I should go back the way I came?

"No, that is the only way I know I shouldn't go," I said to the trees.

Speaking out loud helped me focus and feel alive. It also kept my brain free. I didn't want to think about how lost I was or how badly this could turn out.

I gathered some small rocks, pinecones, and sticks to make an arrow. I pointed it east. Not sure if it was the right choice, but I had to make a decision, and that seemed as good as any. Once the arrow was formed, I hiked in that direction, which wasn't easy. It wasn't like someone had come through and trail blazed for me. I had to work through the thick underbrush and try to stay in a straight line.

Plus, to make things even harder for me, I was in that shapeless dress and barefoot. My feet were cut and sore from the rocks, thorns, and small branches and twigs on the forest floor.

As I went along, I gathered materials to make another arrow, and once I had enough, I stopped and pointed it in the direction I planned to head. I did this for hours. Again, I wasn't sure if I was doing the right thing, but it at least gave me something to do and think about other than the hopeless, helpless way I felt.

I finally came to a creek. It was flowing and clear, and I was oh so thirsty. My head was pounding from a massive headache, and my muscles were cramping from lack of water and the full-body workout of hiking for my life. I knew it was dumb, but I still took a big gulp of water.

"Oh, that's good." I filled my cupped hands over and over. I might pay for this later, but right now, it felt right.

Once I'd drunk my fill, I sat on the bank and tried to decide which way to go from here. Do I follow the current downstream or head upstream?

"Upstream should take me north, which should, in theory, take me to Creekview," I said out loud to no one.

I rested for a few minutes more, dipping my sore feet in the water before gathering up some materials for another directional arrow. I made a clear spot on the bank and placed the items pointing upstream.

Once I was satisfied with my marker, I headed in that direction and hoped I was doing this all right. Can't believe everything you see on television, but it was all I had to hold on to now.

I followed the stream along the bank. It wasn't easy, and I was moving slowly. My brain felt like scrambled eggs, which was probably a combo of lack of water, no food, and little sleep.

But I focused on Oakley and getting back to her safely. I had to. I'd made a promise to her bio mom that I would take care of her. I also thought of my family. I knew from talking to the dead how painful the grief was for those left behind. If at all possible, I wasn't going to do that to them.

"No, Jo, you have too much to live for. Keep going." I said out loud. I pushed on despite the foggy feeling in my head.

After a while, the bank got steep, and clumsy me, I lost my footing. I slid down nearly into the creek.

I squealed as I tumbled and stopped just inches from the water. I tried to stand, but I was so dizzy that I sat there for a moment. That's when I heard what sounded like an engine and someone calling my name.

I listened, almost holding my breath. I quietly climbed back up, trying to stay undercover because I couldn't be sure it wasn't Donovan looking for me.

"Joanna!" The voice called out. The engine sound got closer, and there was a whacking sound.

I tried to see who it was. I knew as it got closer that it wasn't Donovan, but I wasn't clear-headed enough to recognize him.

"Joanna!" The voice was nearly on top of me now, and I still couldn't see him.

I moved farther up the bank and toward the voice. This could be a search party for me, and I couldn't hide forever.

That's when I saw him. It was Al.

"Al! Al, I'm here." I yelled out.

"Joanna?" He cut the engine and was running toward me.

"Oh my gawd, I'm so happy to see you." I fell into his arms. An embarrassing habit I had gotten into when I was in trouble: falling into the arms of men I barely knew. "You have a nice voice."

This was the first time I'd ever heard him speak. It was a rich, deep voice, and I immediately felt safe with him.

"You're safe," he said, looking me over. "I'll call this in."

He grabbed a radio from his waist and told them that he found me. I heard a bunch of voices fighting to be heard in reply.

He loaded me onto his ATV and then climbed on behind me. "Let's get you home, Ms. Joanna."

Chapter Forty-Three

It had been a few days since my rescue. I was barely conscious when Al and I made it back to the rest of the group. The faces were blurs, but I knew my dad was there. He held my hand and wouldn't let go.

They transported me to the hospital, keeping me overnight to rest and rehydrate me. Thankfully, the water I had drunk hadn't made me sick, but I was covered head to toe in scrapes and bruises—some from running blindly through the woods, others from my kidnapper.

I walked down the hall with my dog right by my side. Since coming home, the dog had not let me out of his sight. Honestly, I didn't mind and felt safe knowing he was here.

"You're a good boy," I said to him. "I know you would have saved me if you could have."

He grinned and wagged his tail in reply.

I opened the door to my daughter's room. I was hit with the sweet smell of baby.

"There's my girl," I said to her smiling face.

I was so glad she didn't understand what had happened to me or why I looked like I'd been beaten. Picking her up, I carried her to the changing table.

She smiled and chatted to me. No words yet, still a bit too young, but she was starting to make sounds that I believed would soon be words.

These sweet moments with her made me so thankful he'd been caught and that I was safe. Soon justice would be served for his victims, and the town could breathe a little easier knowing that the Playhouse Killer was behind bars.

Once she was changed, I carried her into the living room so I could feed her. I cooed and talked to her. She listened and replied with her own baby speak. It was times like this that had made me want to survive, to get back to her. I knew I would never take it for granted.

We'd canceled all of my appointments for the next two weeks so I could rest, recover, and have some downtime. I didn't know how long I would take off, but we started with two weeks. It was only another four before our tour, so I might take off until after the tour.

While the clients were disappointed, everyone seemed to be understanding, and I had offered them discounted rates once we got them rescheduled. That seemed to satisfy most.

Oakley finished her bottle, so I settled her on the floor with her toys. She was getting better at scooting and reaching for them. I watched her play and scratched the dog behind his ears.

I was waiting on Clint and Terry. They were coming to check in on me and take my official statement. They'd given me a few days to get home and rest from the ordeal.

After watching the baby for a while, I puttered around doing chores and catching up on emails. Even though I wasn't seeing clients, work didn't stop completely. There were invoices to approve, fan emails to reply to, and proofreading our newsletter.

Finally, there was a knock at the door. It was the detectives.

"Hey, guys. Come in," I said when I opened the door.

"Hey, Jo." They said in near unison.

We went to the living room. Terry was carrying a case. I assumed it was the recording equipment he had mentioned. When they got to the living room, Clint scooped up Oakley.

"Hi, little girl."

She grinned at him and grabbed for his face, her favorite greeting.

"Are y'all ready for this?" Clint asked me.

"Yes, I am."

They got the equipment set up, talked me through the process, and went through some standard questions, like my name and address. Then they got into the meat of it.

"How do you know Donovan Pollack?" Terry asked.

"I hired him to do some projects around my house."

"How long did you know him?" Terry asked.

"About six or seven weeks."

"Can you tell us what happened on the morning of the fifth?"

I told them how he came over, and when I greeted him, he pulled me into the van, continuing my story until Al found me. Some of this was hard to talk about, like the days of playing house in the little mobile home, but overall, I was at peace knowing I was safe at home and he was locked up. I knew we had enough evidence against him that justice would be served, and he would be put away for life.

After a few more questions, it was over.

"Okay, thanks. That was all we needed." Terry said, turning off the recorder. "You good?"

"Yeah, I am." I paused. "Did we ever figure out if the green car that I've seen a few times belonged to him? All I knew was the van."

"Yeah, it was his mom's."

"Ah, okay." That meant that I shouldn't be followed any longer, at least this time, though I hoped there wasn't a next time.

"I'm sorry that we got you wrapped into this," Clint said, still holding the baby. It was heartwarming.

"You didn't get me involved. He was after me from the beginning, so it wouldn't have mattered if y'all asked me to investigate or not."

They both nodded.

"Well, we'll get out of your hair," Terry said as he picked up the equipment.

"Here you go, baby girl." Clint put her back on the floor.

She cooed and kicked before realizing he was walking away. She started crying. I picked her up, laughing.

"She likes you, Clint."

"I see that." He tickled her foot. "Sorry, I have to go, but I'll see you soon."

Terry went out to the car while Clint hung back. He looked at the car and then back at me.

"You know my history with my fiancée." He flashed a weak smile. "When you were lost, I felt like I died a little. I don't know that I can go through this, and there's the baby too. It's a lot of potential pain."

I thought about what Monica had said about him. He was loyal, caring, and when he loved, he loved with his whole heart. I knew I didn't want to be the source of his pain.

"Clint, it's fine. I get it." I put out my hand. "Friends?"

"Friends," he said.

Before you go: If you loved Replicated Murder and haven't already received a copy of Unsolved Murder, the prequel to this series check out my website for the offer for your free novella.

www.ejwheltonwrites.com

Note by the Author:

Thank you for reading my stories.

Writing about a serial killer was a challenge. I had to track each detail and research a lot of different topics. But it was so much fun to write that it hardly seemed like work.

I have so many people to thank for the help with this one, but I'd never do the list justice so just know that all the edits, flow suggestions, word suggestions, etc were all appreciated and taken to heart.

I hope if you have enjoyed the second book in the series and reconnecting with Joanna, Clint, Micah, Tessa and the whole Creekview family, and that you will join for the next book, Organized Murder.

Thank you for your support and happy reading!